Kidnapped . . .

I lost track of where we were as I fought and screamed. I don't think we were more than four or five houses down the street when he turned me toward the back door of a small brick house . . . all of the blinds were drawn.

He pushed open the door and walked me in. The door shut behind me, and I heard him turn the locks.

The house had the feel of a place whose owners were away for a very long time.

Or maybe they were dead. . . .

BE MINE

JANE McFANN

SCHOLASTIC INC.
New York Toronto London Auckland Sydney

No part of this publication may be reproduced in whole or in part, or stored in a retrieval system, or transmitted in any form or by any means, electronic, mechanical, photocopying, recording, or otherwise, without written permission of the publisher. For information regarding permission, write to Scholastic Inc., 730 Broadway, New York, NY 10003.

ISBN 0-590-46690-9

12 11 10 9 8 7 6 5 4 3 2 1   4 5 6 7 8/9

Printed in the U.S.A.   01

First Scholastic printing, January 1994

— To my parents, with gratitude for all that they do to make my life happier and easier.

— And to Judith Cushman Lloyd, for years of friendship and picket fences.

TODAY I SAW HER FOR THE FIRST TIME. I'VE SEEN HER BEFORE, OF COURSE. MANY TIMES. BUT TODAY WAS THE FIRST TIME THAT I REALLY SAW HER. SAW HER BEAUTIFUL EYES, TOUCHED WITH TRACES OF SADNESS. SAW THE LIPS THAT WILL SOON BE SMILING, SMILING AT ME.

TODAY I SAW HER, SAW HER FOR THE FIRST TIME.

AND OUR LIVES WILL NEVER BE THE SAME AGAIN.

Chapter 1

"Starling Horace Whitman the Fifth, put your glasses back on right now!" Starling and I were stretched out on our backs under a huge elm tree on the University of Delaware campus. We were staring up at the leaves. Wait, let me correct that. I was staring at the leaves. Starling was staring at whatever blurred mess was left when he took off his horn-rimmed glasses.

"I like it better this way," Starling protested. "When you're as nearsighted as I am, all you see are patterns of light and darkness. It's like being an Impressionist painter without having to bother with art lessons."

"Starling, I'm beginning to take this personally."

"Exactly what is your problem, Bethany?"

"I feel like you're refusing to wear your

glasses because you don't want to have to endure actually seeing me in vivid detail."

"Come closer," Starling said. "I can see you fine."

"How many fingers am I holding up?" I asked suspiciously.

"Fourteen," Starling answered promptly.

"See, you really can't see," I said.

"Come closer," Starling said, reaching out to grab hold of me. He pulled me over next to him, then lowered his face over mine until our eyelashes brushed.

"There," he said, either deliberately or accidentally crossing his eyes. "I can see you perfectly."

"You're impossible," I said.

"I know," Starling replied. "That's what makes me so adorable."

"Infuriating, impossible, and . . ." I was running out of adjectives.

"Adorable," Starling finished for me. He pulled my head closer and kissed me.

Maybe he was just a *tiny* bit adorable, but I would never admit that to him. He was difficult enough to deal with as it was.

"Starling," I finally said, even though I really was enjoying the kiss.

"Not my name," he said, kissing me again.

"Bird," I said softly.

"Nope," he said. "I get to keep kissing you until you get my name right."

"Ethelbert?" I tried.

"How did you guess?" Starling asked with a sigh, rolling away from me. "I thought it would take you at least an hour to guess that one."

"Just lucky, I guess," I said, smiling at him. "Besides, if we kiss for an hour, how will we ever explain to Mr. Baldwin why we're so late?"

"If we kiss for an hour, we'll have more than that to explain to Mr. Baldwin," Starling said with a leer.

"Yeah, right, Mr. Macho Studmuffin," I said, rumpling his dark brown hair. "You think I'm going to let you ravish my body right here in the middle of campus with thousands of people walking by?"

"If it's only the setting that's bothering you, I can take care of that," Starling said, blinking at me owlishly. "There's quite a nice clump of bushes right over there."

"Come *on*, Starling," I laughed. With a groan, he groped for his glasses and put them on.

"Oh, no, who is this hideous wench I'm

with?" he yelled, staring at me in outrage.

"Starling, Mr. Baldwin is waiting for us."

"Oh, it's you, Bethany."

"I hate your guts. Get up."

Starling lurched to his feet, then reached a hand down to me. I slapped it away and got up without his assistance.

"See if I ever carry your groceries across a street in the snow when you're ninety-seven," Starling said.

You'd think by now I'd be used to Starling's insanity, but he still makes me laugh. We headed toward Dinosaur, his 1968 Plymouth Fury that looks more like a tank than any normal vehicle on the roads these days.

"Do you think Mr. Baldwin will make it back to school this year?" I asked Starling, jogging a little to keep up with his long strides.

Mr. Baldwin, our history teacher, had a pretty bad heart attack back in the winter. Actually, he had it while Starling, Rocco, Herbert, Jyl, and I were trapped in our high school with him during an ice storm. We got him help as soon as we could, and after weeks in the hospital, he had finally been allowed to come home. Starling and I both believed that he wasn't ready to be released yet, but he had given the nurses such a hard time that they probably forced his doctor to get him out. He had a visiting nurse that came to his house for a while, but he ran her out, too. Now Starling and I stop by to see him every day after school. We get his groceries and do any errands he thinks up. He putters around and does some of his own cooking and cleaning. We do the rest.

He fusses and yells and complains at us all the time, but it's just his way. We know that he's glad to see us.

"I don't know if he'll make it back before graduation or not," Starling said. Mr. Baldwin had planned to retire in June, which is when Starling and I graduate.

"I hope he does, but I'm worried that it would be too much for him," I said.

"You worry too much," Starling said. "You know Mr. Baldwin. He's too contrary to die."

"I still worry," I said.

The good thing about Starling is he knows when to be serious. My mother died very suddenly, and Starling realizes that death is not one of my favorite subjects. He pulled me to his side, draping his arm around my shoulders. "It's okay, Beach," he said.

I used to hate it when he called me that. I'm named after Bethany Beach in southern

Delaware, and he nicknamed me "Beach" after I started calling him "Bird." Now I'm so used to it that it seems normal.

We were both quiet as Starling drove to Mr. Baldwin's house. We usually went straight there after school, but today was such a beautiful, almost-summer day that we had detoured past campus. Suddenly I was worried.

"What if Mr. Baldwin thinks something happened to us?" I asked. I couldn't keep my worries to myself any longer.

"He knows you'll take care of me," Starling said.

"Are you mocking my independence?" I asked, turning to look at him.

"No, I'm celebrating it," Starling replied with a perfectly straight face.

"*Star*ling," I said, with a definite note of warning in my voice.

"Yes, dear?" he asked meekly.

"Cut the crap," I said. "You know you never give in to me like that."

"I'm waiting for you to give in to me," he said with an attempt at an evil chuckle.

"You never give up, do you?" I asked.

"Never," he said. "Now get your hormones under control before we see Mr. Baldwin. I don't want you panting in front of him."

"My hormones? *My* hormones?" I shrieked.

"I don't hear *me* making suggestive comments all the time."

"Ah, you shameless hussy," Starling said. "Trying to take advantage of me right there in the middle of campus. Kissing me until I had to fight you off in outrage and embarrassment. Sometimes I wonder if you weren't raised by wolves rather than by civilized human beings."

"Starling — "

"Stop," he ordered. "I can't take any more of your demands right now. I'm exhausted. I don't know how much longer I can endure being treated as a mere sex object."

"Starling Horace . . ."

"We're here. Smile sweetly for Mr. Baldwin. He's staring out the window at us."

I turned and waved to Mr. Baldwin, who disappeared from the window. Shortly afterward, the front door opened.

"No, Bethany, I will not make mad, passionate love to you right here in broad daylight. Have you no sense of decency?" Starling proclaimed loudly. Thank heavens we were still in the car.

I clapped my hand over his mouth, staring at Mr. Baldwin in his doorway. He now had his storm door open. I couldn't tell from his expression whether he had heard Starling. I fervently hoped not.

"Starling, you're going to pay for this," I hissed, cautiously taking my hand away from his mouth but ready to slap it back if Starling started yelling again.

"I certainly hope so," he said, reaching over and patting my knee.

Chapter 2

"Hi, Mr. Baldwin. Sorry we're late." I'd rushed up to the door before Starling could cause any more difficulty.

"And what caused your tardy arrival?" Mr. Baldwin snapped. "Hordes of Visigoths blocking traffic, perhaps?"

"Actually, I think they were Huns," Starling said. He'd finally made it to the front door.

"I see," Mr. Baldwin said gruffly. "Come in. Come in."

If I hadn't spent so much time with him, I would have been offended by the reception. I know Mr. Baldwin, though, and I know that's just his way. Actually, I'd be worried if he were really nice to us. Then I'd know he was sick.

"Who gave you the flowers?" I asked when we were in Mr. Baldwin's living room. That place is usually decorated with nothing more festive than the covers of the stacks of books that are piled on most of the flat surfaces. Today, however, there were some crisp yellow daffodils in a drinking glass.

Mr. Baldwin mumbled some response, turning his back to us.

"What was that?" Starling asked brightly.

"They were brought here without my invitation or desire by some interfering woman who thinks she is a messenger of good will and Christian charity," Mr. Baldwin finally said sharply.

"Somebody from the local church?" I translated.

"Yes. I have absolutely no idea how she got my name," Mr. Baldwin said. "Those church types must hover about the hospital like buzzards, looking for the unfortunate souls who are forced to seek help from modern medicine."

"I doubt that she came here to hover over you like a buzzard," Starling said, trying not to smile.

"Then perhaps she was a real estate agent taking a look at how close to death I am so that she can put my house on the market before my corpse has even cooled."

I didn't like this talk about buzzards and corpses. "Then she was sadly mistaken," I said quickly. "You aren't going to be a corpse for many, many years yet."

"Is that so, Miss Anderson?" Mr. Baldwin said.

"Yes, it is," I said firmly.

"And what is the source of this prophecy?"

"You are," I said. "Just a few weeks ago, you couldn't get out of bed for more than a few minutes without getting pale and shaky. Now you're ready to take on any visitors, and had enough strength to be so contrary with the visiting nurse that she refuses to come back."

"The woman was a moron," Mr. Baldwin said firmly.

"Why?" I asked. "Because she told you to watch your diet and limit your stress and take walks?"

"I already limit my diet to foods I enjoy, and the stress of teaching impossible young people is my job, and I will not take walks like some trained show dog on the end of some nurse's leash."

"Exercise is important in your recovery," Starling said, jumping in to help me. Mr. Baldwin was being extremely difficult.

"I exercise," Mr. Baldwin said.

"How? Where?" Starling said. Normally neither of us would be so forceful with Mr. Baldwin, but we were worried about him.

"I walk inside the house," Mr. Baldwin said. "It is one hundred fifty-seven steps to enter and cross every room on this level, and there are fourteen steps to the second floor, which I climb and descend at least four times a day. Does that suffice, young Doctor Whitman?"

"No," Starling said.

"And what, pray tell, is your objection?" Mr. Baldwin asked. I tried to send a mental warning to Starling to back off since the perpetually sharp edge to Mr. Baldwin's voice was now about ready to slice to the bone.

"You need fresh air," Starling replied earnestly. "You need to walk a certain distance each day, and then gradually increase it in both aerobic intensity and duration."

"You sound like you want to put me in tights and have me prance around to music," Mr. Baldwin said in disbelief. "Besides, I have always believed that fresh air is vastly overrated. In fact, I'm not sure it even exists these days. Pollution has destroyed it. Are you advocating that I go out and breathe the fluorocarbons discharged by the millions of cans of hair spray that young girls use these days?"

How can you argue with a man like that? I patted my hair absentmindedly, glad for once that it was in its normal disarray rather than sprayed into order by chemical pollutants.

I was afraid that Starling was going to continue this argument, and it definitely wasn't heading in a very good direction. "What do you want for dinner?" I asked abruptly.

"A thick steak marbled with fat pan-fried in butter with fried potatoes and chocolate cake," Mr. Baldwin said fretfully.

He was being obstinate. Starling and I do his grocery shopping every Friday, and we carefully check what he wants against the sheets the hospital sent home on dietary restrictions.

I went into the kitchen and left Starling to deal with Mr. Baldwin. I love his kitchen. There are two big windows in it, and two of the walls have a wonderful maple paneling that is rich and reddish from years of polish and cooking smoke. I surveyed what was left from the last shopping trip and went back into the living room, where Starling was holding forth on the dangers of cholesterol.

"A baked chicken breast with herbs, green beans with lemon juice, a small baked potato with unflavored yogurt, and peaches in their own juice for dessert," I said firmly.

"The trouble with those of you who want to save the earth is that you make it so boring that it isn't worth living on it," Mr. Baldwin said peevishly. Still, if you looked very closely, there was a hint of a smile on his face.

I truly believe that he isn't as bad as he sounds. I have to believe that.

We managed to get Mr. Baldwin interested in a historical documentary on one of the educational channels, and then Starling and I went to fix dinner.

We argued about what temperature to bake the chicken, and I literally had to grab the potato out of Starling's hand and stab it repeatedly to discourage him from putting it into the microwave without piercing it just to see if it really would explode.

I also fell for Starling's lie that he couldn't find the peaches in the pantry, and when I got there he kissed me in the canned goods.

He seems to have this thing about small, cramped places. The first significant time we spent together was in a closet. Starling Horace Whitman the Fifth. Who will ever understand him?

He *is* cute when his glasses steam up, though.

The three of us debated the role of oil in the international economy while Mr. Baldwin ate, and then Starling and I got ready to leave.

"Take those flowers with you, Miss Anderson," Mr. Baldwin said as we were on our way out.

"No, they're yours," I said. "They look pretty here."

"Then I'll simply throw them out," he said.

"No," I said. "I want to be able to enjoy them when I come here tomorrow."

"Then the two of you will be stopping by, I might assume?" he asked.

"Of course we will," Starling said.

Perhaps it was the fading light, but Mr. Baldwin looked relieved. "I suppose I'll have to endure that," he said.

Starling and I walked to his car in silence. It was only when we were headed toward my house that I spoke.

"It makes me so sad that we are the only people he has," I said.

"Why?" Starling asked.

"He should have family or friends or something," I said.

"We're his friends," Starling said.

"Yes, but we're just kids," I said. "Shouldn't he have some people his own age to talk to, or children or grandchildren?"

"Not everyone ends up with the all-American family including a spouse, 2.5 kids, a house in the suburbs, and a dog named Spot," Starling said.

"That's *it*!" I yelled.

"What's it?" Starling asked, blinking at me in confusion.

"A dog!"

"Excuse me?" Starling said.

"If we got him a dog, he'd have to go for walks," I said. "We have to get Mr. Baldwin a dog."

"How do we even know he likes dogs?" Starling asked.

"How do we know he likes anything?" I said. "Sometimes I'm not even sure he likes us."

"He does," Starling reassured me.

"How do you know?" I asked.

"How could he not like us?" Starling said. "I'm adorable, and you're impossible. What's not to like?"

"Starling, I am not impossible."

"Then why haven't we had mad, passionate sex in some remote location or the backseat of Dinosaur, whichever comes first?"

"Starling, a dog," I said, trying to get him back to the proper topic.

"I will not have sex with a dog," Starling said in outrage. "I do have my standards, you know."

I blushed, and I knew Starling saw it, which made me blush even more. "That's not what I mean, and you know it."

"A dog," Starling said. "We need to give this some more thought before we do anything rash."

"Starling, we're talking about getting Mr. Baldwin a pet, not about changing the course of history."

"What kind of dog did you have in mind?" Starling asked. "Not that I'm agreeing to this, you understand."

"Something little and cute," I said.

"For Mr. Baldwin?" Starling asked. "How about a pit bull?"

YESTERDAY I THOUGHT HER HAIR WAS
  BROWN.
TODAY I KNOW THAT THE BROWN IS
  TOUCHED WITH RED LIKE THE FUR
  OF SOME EXOTIC FOX THAT LIVES IN
  THE DEEP WOODS.

YESTERDAY I THOUGHT HER EYES
  WERE BROWN.
TODAY I KNOW THAT THE BROWN IS
  CIRCLED WITH GREEN, THE GREEN
  OF AN EMERALD BARELY LIT WITH
  THE FLAME OF A SINGLE CANDLE.

YESTERDAY I THOUGHT SHE WAS
  BEAUTIFUL.
TODAY I KNOW THAT SHE DEFINES ALL
  THAT IS BEAUTIFUL IN THE WORLD.

TOMORROW I WILL LOOK AGAIN INTO
  THOSE EYES, AND I WILL BE HAPPY
  FOR THE FIRST TIME.

SHE WILL MAKE ME HAPPY. SHE MUST.

IT IS HER DESTINY, AND SHE MUST
  FULFILL IT.

Chapter 3

Starling drove me home and then kept me company while I began dinner for my father and me. I sure am getting enough practice cooking these days. Actually, I've done a lot of that kind of thing ever since my mother died. So I'm not complaining. It's good to know that I can run a household, although my dad does his part with chores on the weekend.

But he's been less help than usual these days. It seems that the company he now works for is being sued for possible copyright infringement for some process that is really important in the division he works in, and he's been under a lot of pressure. He has had to research the background of the process and when the company started using it and all that kind of stuff, which is pretty complicated since it happened years and years before he started working there. The result has been a lot of overtime, even on weekends, and a rather grumpy father.

I have to admit that my father's bad moods have made me enjoy Starling more than usual. The boy is almost constantly in a good mood, something I find amazing. The best part is that his moods are genuine, not some faked pseudo-good cheer that would make me want to throw up. Starling has the true and unusual talent of being entertained by life. Everything is a toy to him, a game to be invented. It's pretty amazing.

Take, for example, walking from the car to the kitchen door and going into the house. Now with most people, that would seem rather mundane, but with Starling, it's an adventure:

"The destination lurks ahead, resonant with waves of dark danger that fill the air with the cries of bats rabid for human blood," Starling declaimed in his deepest, most rounded yet hushed tones as we pulled up in front of my house. Sitting there was a perfectly cheerful suburban house that even had a few flowers poking up around the bushes.

"Right, Starling. I don't have time to play. Are you going to help me start dinner?"

Starling eased his car door open inch by careful inch, then flung himself out on the pavement on his knees and crouched below window level. "I'll cover you while you open your door," he hissed. "Watch out for angry munchkins."

"Okay," I said, flinging open my door and stepping out.

"Down," Starling shouted, duck-walking around the car to my side, grabbing my shoulder, and pushing me down.

Luckily, I really don't care what the neighbors think.

"Come on, Starling," I said, shrugging off his hand and starting up the driveway.

"I'll save you despite your wanton disregard for personal safety," Starling yelled, racing up the driveway, darting left and right, doing ninja stances and karate yells at every bush and tree.

I took out my keys and started to unlock the kitchen door. Starling threw his body between me and the door.

"Wait. I'll absorb the brunt of the explosion with my brawn," he said. "Let me say one brief prayer before battle."

"Starling, will you move so I can open the door?"

"Protect the innocent, whatever powers look down upon those named for beaches and other geographical landmarks. Let them live, that they may someday repent their lack of gratitude."

"Starling, I'll be very grateful if you'll let me unlock the door and start dinner before my retired Army father, who knows how to handle every weapon ever created, comes home to ask why you're holding his only daughter hostage outside the kitchen door."

Threatening him with my father works every time.

"How grateful?" he asked.

"This grateful," I said, slipping inside the door and shutting it before he could follow me in. I locked it, then made the mistake of pulling back the curtain on the door to look out. There was Starling, face plastered against the glass, lips and nose flattened, eyes bulging.

"Get in here," I said, almost knocking him over as I threw open the door.

"Ah-ha," he said, "it's pity that works. And here I've been wasting all of this time being strong and brave."

"You know, Starling, we really should get Mr. Baldwin a dog. Haven't you read those studies that show that older people with pets are healthier and live longer?" I opened the refrigerator and surveyed the contents. Goulash. The hamburger was already thawed and there was one onion left. I put the hamburger on the kitchen counter along with the onion, then grabbed macaroni and tomato sauce from the pantry. Starling had his head and shoulders buried in the refrigerator. He finally came out with an apple, which he was welcome to. I hate apples unless it's October and they're fresh from the orchard.

"Bethany, those studies are about normal older people, not Mr. Baldwin."

"What's abnormal about him?" I asked.

"Well, he's not exactly the type to sit in a rocking chair on the front porch watching the cars go by and scratching the head of his faithful dog Rover," Starling said, biting into the apple, which squished instead of crunched. Yuck.

"True. His idea of fun is tormenting five classes a day of high school students," I admitted. Mr. Baldwin is a school legend for pop quizzes, difficult tests, and demanding standards. Still, I have to admit he's the best teacher I've ever had.

"So why torture a dog with him?" Starling asked.

"Because deep down he has a soft heart," I said. "You know that. After all, why would we spend so much time with him if he didn't?"

"It's obviously displacement activity," Starling said seriously. "What you really want to do is make love with me, but since you are determined to fight your irresistible attraction to one of the most attractive young men in the world, you spend your time in the company of an old man who will chaperone us and prevent you from attacking me."

"Right, Starling. Do you really want to be my hero?"

"Yes, of course. Shall I slay dragons? Scale cliffs with only my fingernails and toenails between me and the rocks 8,563 feet below?"

"How about chopping this onion for me?"

"Sure you wouldn't prefer a dragon?"

"Nope. Sorry."

"Okay," Starling said. He rummaged in the refrigerator again and came out with a slice of white bread, which he ripped into quarters.

"Starling, I want you to chop the onion, not make stuffing."

"O ye of little faith," Starling said, stuffing all the bread into his mouth, some of it hanging out.

"You're disgusting. What is this?" I said, getting out a pot in which to boil water for the macaroni.

"Watch. The latest advance in scientific knowledge." Starling got out a knife and proceeded to take the skin off the onion and chop it, all the time with the bread dangling out of his mouth. He looked ridiculous.

"Notice anything?" he asked when he was almost finished, his voice muffled by the bread.

"Other than the fact that you look like a fool?" I said.

He finished the onion and swept it into the frying pan that I had put beside him. He took out the bread, which was a rather disgusting gooey mass.

"Look me in the eyes," he said.

"Starling, I don't have time for this. I have to finish dinner."

"Seriously, Bethany, look."

He had chopped the onion for me, so I looked. All I saw were two familiar brown eyes behind his glasses.

"No tears!" he proclaimed triumphantly.

He was right. There wasn't even a hint of redness.

"I read somewhere that if you put bread in your mouth, your eyes aren't irritated by chopping onions," he said.

I had to admit that was pretty amazing. I humored him by giving him the jar of sauce to open. He likes it when he has a chance to look big and strong. His face turned red, and veins bulged at his temples before he got the jar open, but I pretended I hadn't seen.

By the time the macaroni was boiled and

drained and added to the browned hamburger and onion along with the tomato sauce, my father was home. Luckily, he likes Starling, and he invited him to stay for dinner.

I was glad he did, because my father seemed very preoccupied, which was almost worse than his being grumpy. Starling kept the conversation going by talking to him about the evil ways of lawyers, a popular subject these days with my father.

I was eating my goulash and feeling a little left out when the phone rang. I got up to answer it.

"Bethany? I hate to disturb you, but I'm trying to find Starling and I thought you might be able to help me."

"Hello, Jyl," I said with a sigh. Jyl was with us when the ice storm trapped us, and we chat at school. She seems all right, but I still don't trust her fully. Especially when it comes to Starling.

"He's right here," I said. "I'll get him."

"Thanks, Beth," Jyl said. I hate to be called that. I think she knows it.

"Starling, telephone," I called into the dining room.

"If it's my parents, tell them that you held me hostage and refused to let me come home," Starling hissed.

"It's Jyl," I said.

Starling got a huge, silly grin on his face. "Oh."

I threw the telephone at him. I went back into the dining room and almost yelled at my father when he started talking about work again. How was I supposed to hear what Starling was saying?

There must not have been much to hear. Starling was back in record time.

"That was Jyl," he said.

"I know," I said.

I nearly exploded in the silence that followed. I thought I could wait him out, but I couldn't.

"What did she want?" I asked sweetly.

"She's stuck on the physics homework."

All three of us were in the same class. "Why didn't she ask me?" I asked, still trying to sound calm.

"I don't know," Starling said, the picture of innocence. "Great dinner. I really need to go now. Nice to see you as always, Mr. Anderson."

I followed Starling from the table to the kitchen door and then out into the driveway.

"Jyl snaps her fingers and you run?" I asked snidely.

"Something like that," Starling said. "Thanks for dinner."

I wanted to be nonchalant and unconcerned. I wanted to be above petty jealousy. I wanted to smile sweetly at Starling, give him a hug, and send him on his way.

All I managed to do was turn my back and walk back into the house.

Forget getting Mr. Baldwin a dog.

I'd get one for myself.

Had to be better than dealing with a fickle, impossible, hormone-ridden boy.

I MUST APPROACH HER SLOWLY AND CAREFULLY AND QUIETLY, AS A HUNTER WOULD A DEER ON THE EDGE OF THE FIELD.

I MUST BE NOISELESS AND PATIENT, READY TO DISAPPEAR, KNOWING THAT I WILL NEVER REALLY DISAPPEAR. SHE IS A PART OF ME NOW, AND I COULD NO MORE LEAVE HER THAN I COULD CUT OUT MY HEART AND CONTINUE TO LIVE.

GENTLY, QUIETLY, YET PERSISTENTLY, I MUST COME CLOSER AND CLOSER, NEVER CLOSE ENOUGH TO SCARE HER AWAY, BUT CLOSE ENOUGH FOR HER TO START TO REALIZE THAT I EXIST, AND THAT I WILL ALWAYS EXIST FOR HER.

SHE IS ALL THAT IS BEAUTIFUL IN MY LIFE, AND I WILL DO EVERYTHING IN MY POWER TO REPAY HER FOR THAT BEAUTY.

SOON NOW. SOON. THE WAITING WILL BE OVER.

Chapter 4

"Thank you," I said to Starling when I saw him right after homeroom the next morning.

"You're welcome," he said, "but which of my wonderful qualities are you thanking me for at the moment?"

"Don't play dumb with me, Starling. I'm thanking you for the present."

"Which present?" he asked. "My continuing presence in your life? The lilt of laughter I add to your mundane existence? The standard of academic excellence that I set for you on a daily basis? Those presents?"

"Starling, stop. I mean the hearts."

"Hey, I'm not humble. You want to give me credit for the hearts, I'll take it."

"The hearts on my locker, silly," I said. "That really was a cheerful touch for a Monday morning. Thanks." I gave him a quick kiss on the cheek. "I guess that was your way of saying you're sorry for rushing off when Jyl called." I started off toward class.

"Hearts?" I heard Starling repeat. "Sorry?"

He really is thoughtful — most of the time.

At the end of first period, I went to my locker to dump off one book and get another, and there was Starling. You know how guys are. I figured he wanted to admire his handiwork. I mean, it was only three or four of those little gummed hearts that come on sheets, stuck to the top right corner of my locker door. Still, Starling wasn't known for his artistic endeavors, so this was a breakthrough of sorts for him.

"Yes, Starling," I said. "Nice hearts. Nice arrangement. Could you move so that I can get my locker open?"

"I'd really like to take credit," Starling said, "but you know how honest I am, and I just can't let you delude yourself."

"Right, Starling," I said sarcastically, hip-checking him aside so that I could work the combination lock.

"Not my hearts," he said.

I looked at him, and the serious expression on his face told me that he wasn't playing games this time. Still, it was only a few gummed hearts. It wasn't worth any big deal.

"No?" I said. "How interesting. Must be

someone else who thinks I'm wonderful." Normally I wouldn't have said that, but I was still a little ticked off about Jyl.

"Who do you figure it might be?" Starling asked. I tried desperately to hear jealousy in his voice, but it was a stretch.

"Which one is a better question," I said. "See you."

There. Let him see how it felt.

Unfortunately, I can't sustain those situations. By the time Starling and I were in third-period physics together, I didn't have any desire to torment him. Besides, I hadn't been able to finish the last homework problem, and I wanted him to explain it to me before class started.

Unfortunately, someone beat me to his photographic memory.

Jyl was sitting in my seat at the back table next to Starling. Actually, she had pulled the chair so close that she was practically sitting on Starling. She was cuddled up to him as if she were in Antarctica and he was the last ember in a dying fire.

I stood beside her, glaring.

"Oh, Beth," she finally said after my glare should have penetrated at least to her pancreas. "Why don't you just go sit in my seat for a while?"

She might as well have added "like a good little girl" or patted me on the head. Instead, she bent back to Starling. "Okay, Einstein," she said to him. "Wait," she giggled. "Don't take that the wrong way. You're much better-looking than Einstein. What was that next step you were showing me?"

If she were standing on the edge of a cliff that fell into a raging river full of jagged rocks, I'd show her the next step. I stood there for another moment, waiting for Starling to acknowledge me, but Mr. Better-looking-than-Einstein was otherwise occupied.

I sat down in Jyl's seat so hard that it's a wonder the chair survived.

In every problem in physics that period, I substituted Jyl for whatever object had the greatest momentum and seemed to have the best chance for destruction.

Starling came after me when I left class. "Hey, Beach, want to — "

"Knee you in the groin and double you over in pain?" I finished for him. "Yes, *please*."

Reflexively he lowered his books like a shield. "What seems to be your problem?" he asked.

"*My* problem?" I snapped. "I think you're the one with the problem. Or maybe it's not a problem. Maybe you've made your choice."

"This really isn't going well," Starling said.

"Oh, I don't know about that. I'd say that Jyl thinks it's going just fine," I said. I hadn't really wanted to say her name, but it just slipped out.

"Bethany, you're jealous."

"No, I'm not," I said, hoping for the one-in-a-thousand chance that he'd believe me. "I really don't like being asked not to sit in my own seat."

"I was wondering why you were over on the other side of the room," Starling said.

"Because Jyl kicked me there," I answered.

"When?" Starling said, looking puzzled.

"When I came over before class," I said.

"I didn't even notice," Starling said.

"I know, Einstein."

Starling's memory seemed to be drifting back. "I was supposed to hurl Jyl out of your seat, tell her never to even look at me again, and then wipe off the chair before you sat down on it?" he asked.

He was making me feel ridiculous, and I didn't like it one little bit. Still, I'd always sworn never to be the jealous female type.

"Forget it," I said.

"Forget what?" Starling asked. "Besides, we have something much more interesting to talk about."

"What's that?" I asked.

"Sex."

"Starling."

"Okay, that idea you had."

"Which one?"

"The good one."

I knew that Starling was baiting me, and I refused to give in to it.

"Ah, yes, that one. What is there to discuss?"

"Meet me at your house after school, and I'll show you," he said.

I started to ask him about lunch and the other two classes that we had together, but he disappeared.

He also disappeared from lunch and his afternoon classes.

Leave it to Starling to totally confuse me.

When I went to my locker at the end of the day, the three red hearts seemed to be shining in the reflection of the ceiling lights. I smiled at them.

After all, I was going to meet Starling.

I was going to meet Starling. Not Jyl.

Sure enough, there was Starling's huge Plymouth Fury sitting in front of my house. Starling was sprawled across the hood, arms crossed behind his head, eyes closed.

"I can't imagine why somebody hasn't asked you to model for the next hood ornament," I said, walking over to him and putting my hand on his chest. It was warm from the sun.

"Do I look like a bronzed California beach god yet?" Starling asked.

I studied him carefully. There wasn't even a hint of pink on his winter-pale face. "I think you need to bake a little longer," I said.

"You make me sound like cookie dough," Starling said with an exaggerated whine.

Great. Jyl called him a genius, and I called him a Pillsbury reject.

"Where were you all afternoon?" I asked, changing the subject.

"At the dentist," he answered.

"Why didn't you just tell me that at school?" I asked.

"A man needs an aura of mystery," Starling said coyly, striking another pose on the hood.

"Okay, what's the plan?" I asked him, unwilling to pursue this line of reasoning.

"I've given this a great deal of thought," Starling said, sliding rather gracelessly off the hood of Dinosaur. "I don't think I can father your love child."

"Starling!"

"Get in the car, you shameless hussy," Starling said.

"That's more like it," I said, opening the door.

I knew better than to ask him where we were going. Instead, I just turned up the car radio, closed my eyes, and relaxed. It was hard to believe. A few more weeks and Starling and I would graduate from high school. The thought of getting away from high school and all its weirdness made me ecstatic. I'd been ready to leave all of that behind from about the first day of ninth grade.

"Wake up," Starling finally said as he pulled to a stop.

"I'm not asleep," I said curtly. I didn't mean to snap at Starling, but I was in a bit of a funk. I had been dozing. Dreams of small red hearts danced in my mind. One of the hearts seemed to be dripping blood that formed into roses, but it was all a little hazy.

"Are you okay?" Starling looked concerned.

When I saw the front of the building that was facing me, my mind cleared and I smiled broadly. "This *was* my idea, wasn't it?"

"Just remember that." Starling turned away from me and opened his door.

Chapter 5

"Before we go in, we need to agree on some rules," Starling said, stopping me as I reached for the door handle.

"Come on, Starling," I said impatiently.

"This is just a scouting foray," Starling said. "We are not, I repeat not, making any decisions today."

"Sure. Whatever you say. Let's go."

"Bethany, I'm serious. We're just here to look. We can't rush into something like this."

"Starling, stop stalling. Let's go."

With a sigh, Starling pulled open the door. In the reception area, a middle-aged woman with her hair pulled back in an untidy bun smiled at us. "Welcome to the SPCA," she said. "May I help you?"

"We're here to look at dogs," Starling said.

"We're here to adopt a puppy," I said a little too forcefully.

The lady looked a little confused. "Well, let me understand this," she said. "You're either here to look at or adopt a dog or a puppy." She smiled tentatively.

"Right," I said brightly.

"Are you eighteen?" she inquired.

"Yes," I said.

"No," Starling said over my voice.

"You always have had a thing for older women, haven't you, Starling?" I asked sweetly. My birthday was last month; his was later in June.

"And your name is?" She looked at me, dismissing Starling as a child, I suppose.

"We're just here to look," Starling said.

"Bethany Anderson," I said.

The lady looked at us in amazement. I guess if we were comedians she would have told us to work on our timing.

"Come with me," she said. "Now did you have something special in mind?"

"A good-sized dog with a strong personality," Starling said.

"A sweet little puppy," I said, our words overlapping.

"Why don't I just let you look around in the area where we keep our canines. I'll be right over here if you want me to get an animal out for you."

We walked past cage after cage, and my mood immediately changed. I guess Starling had known this would happen because he immediately took my hand, a look of foreboding on his face.

"Oh, Starling," I said as I looked at dog after dog.

"You can't save them all, Bethany," he said.

"But they're in cages. Look at them. They need to run and play and be cuddled."

"Maybe this wasn't such a good idea after all," Starling said. "It's just that I gave a lot of thought to what you said about Mr. Baldwin needing motivation to get out and walk. He certainly needs more company than we can provide, and he chases away all the other humans. I thought maybe a dog would be a good idea."

"I still believe that," I said. I tore my eyes away from a dog that was largely German shepherd and kept walking.

"I thought that maybe if we got some sense of what was available, we could then start to work on Mr. Baldwin, break the idea to him, convince him that there was this really great animal in need of help."

"Starling, you don't have to convince me."

Then it happened. I looked into a pair of brown eyes with bristly eyebrows and stubby eyelashes. I sat right down on the cement floor and stuck my hand through the wire cage toward a strange-looking runt of a puppy. Its hair stuck out in all directions as if it were nothing but cowlicks, and it was a mottled brown and white and gray. It was definitely part terrier, but there was something else in it, too. Cocker spaniel? Poodle? I couldn't tell. The puppy sat right where it was and stared seriously at my finger, not licking it, but not backing away, either.

"Oh no," Starling said, bending down beside me. "Not right at all. Too small. Too ugly. Definitely not tough enough."

"How dare you call him ugly?" I said. "He's got character." I turned around to where the woman was standing and beckoned for her.

"No," Starling said. "We're just *looking*, remember?"

"I just want a better look," I said. Starling muttered something under his breath.

"Yes?" the lady said.

"May I see this one?" I said sweetly, pointing to the motionless puppy.

"He's a young one," the lady said. "Somebody left him on our doorstep a few days ago. I don't think he's quite adjusted yet. But he's healthy," she said, opening the cage door. The puppy stood up and stared out.

"Come here," I crooned softly, holding out my hand. The puppy moved toward me with careful steps, his nose quivering. He sniffed at my finger and then sneezed loudly, nearly losing his balance. Starling sat down beside me and laughed. The puppy turned to look at him, then took a few careful steps toward Starling. Starling held out his hand and the puppy sniffed it, then chomped down on one finger. He didn't do it with vicious intensity; he just bit down with his sharp little puppy teeth. Proudly he turned around and marched back to me. He put his front feet up on my leg and stared up at me soulfully. Then he gave a very soft little yip.

"I've never heard him make a sound before," the lady said. "I guess he's finally finding his voice."

"And his teeth," Starling said, rubbing his finger.

I carefully put out my hands and let the puppy sniff them, then gently picked him up and held him against my chest. The puppy immediately nuzzled against me and began to fall asleep.

"This is not good," Starling said. He reached for the puppy. Before he could take him away from me, the puppy growled, not even opening his eyes.

"He knows your scent already," I said. "Good dog," I crooned.

"Bethany," Starling said.

"He's perfect," I said, holding the puppy tighter.

"How do you figure that?" Starling said.

"He likes me and he bit you," I said. "He's obviously a perfect judge of character."

"But we're looking for a bigger, older dog that will get Mr. Baldwin out and around," Starling protested.

"This one is perfect," I said. "He's just feisty enough to hold his own. Besides, look at him. Even Mr. Baldwin couldn't resist that face."

"We'll see about that," Starling said. "Okay, put him back and we'll go talk to Mr. Baldwin."

"No," I said, looking at him in amazement. "I will not put him back."

"You agreed," Starling said. "We're just looking today. We need to get Mr. Baldwin's approval before we do anything else."

"I am not putting this puppy back," I said firmly.

"Look, we'll talk to Mr. Baldwin today, and if he agrees, we'll come back tomorrow," Starling said.

"There is no way on the face of the earth that I'm going to let this sweet little thing spend one more night in this cold wire cage," I said.

"Bethany, be reasonable."

"No," I said, getting up from the floor. "I want this puppy," I said to the lady as I crossed the room.

"There's some paperwork we need to complete," she said, looking from me to Starling and back again.

"Bethany," Starling said, "let's think about . . ."

"Will you hold the puppy while I sign these?" I said firmly, handing him the dog while I sat down at the desk in front of the lady.

Starling took the puppy rather gingerly. It opened its eyes and stared up at Starling, giving a tentative growl.

"It's okay," I said. "Uncle Starling won't hurt you, even though he does want to leave you here." The puppy growled a little louder.

"Thanks a lot," Starling said. "He'll probably grow up to track me down and rip out my throat while I sleep."

"Oh, I don't think he'll get that big," the lady behind the desk said, looking at Starling.

"He's not serious," I said, trying to get the papers finished as quickly as possible before the lady decided that anybody in the company of a lunatic like Starling wasn't fit to adopt a puppy.

Starling snorted and went outside to wait. I knew that deep down he was as won over by the puppy as I was, but he just couldn't gracefully accept that his rules had been so quickly and thoroughly overturned.

As we made our way back toward Newark, I made Starling stop at the pet store, giving him every cent I had and telling him to get whatever the puppy needed. He came back with a bulky bag. As we headed toward Mr. Baldwin's, I inventoried the contents. Food, two bowls, a collar and leash, some toys, and a small bed. The puppy was sleeping peacefully on my lap.

Starling stopped the car, pulling over a block away from Mr. Baldwin's. "Okay, so what's your plan?" he said pointedly.

"What do you mean, my plan?" I asked.

"How are you going to get Mr. Baldwin to accept that pitiful excuse of a puppy?"

"Just drive," I said. "You'll think of something."

"Oh, no, you don't," Starling began.

"I think the puppy needs to go to the bathroom," I announced.

"Not in my car," Starling yelled.

"Then drive," I said.

With a sudden burst of speed, Starling got us to Mr. Baldwin's. I got out, putting the puppy on the grass, where he promptly peed.

"Told you so," I said smugly.

"Show's about to begin," Starling said, pointing to the front door. There stood Mr. Baldwin, looking none too pleased at the vision of a small puppy using his front lawn.

"I'll be at home," Starling said. "Call me when you're ready for a ride to your house."

He started to get back in his car.

"Don't you dare," I hissed.

"This is *your* idea," he hissed back. "You deal with it."

"Starling, you have to help," I whispered. "We have to convince Mr. Baldwin to keep him."

"You convince him," Starling said, opening the car door and slipping behind the wheel.

"Starling Horace Whitman the Fifth," I whispered desperately, turning to wave to Mr. Baldwin, who now had the screen door open and looked ready to come out.

"What's it worth to you?" Starling asked.

"A lot," I said desperately.

"How much?" Starling said calmly.

"Can't we negotiate later?" I said, glancing at Mr. Baldwin, who seemed ready to attack.

"Now's a much better time," Starling said.

"What do you want?" I asked, knowing I was making a mistake, but not seeing any other way out.

"Ah, how long I've waited to hear you beg," Starling said.

"I didn't mean *that*," I said abruptly.

"I know," Starling said with a sigh. "My car is looking a little dirty."

"I'll wash it."

"And a little dull."

"I'll wax it."

"And . . ."

"Starling, Mr. Baldwin is coming toward us."

"Okay, okay. I'll help you." Starling bounded out of the car and came to stand beside me. I scooped up the puppy and together the three of us faced Mr. Baldwin.

Chapter 6

"And what is your reason for having this pitiful excuse for a canine, if I dare defame the species, void its bladder on *my* lawn?" bellowed Mr. Baldwin.

The puppy cocked his head and looked at Mr. Baldwin, who was now out on his front step.

I took a deep breath and picked up the puppy. "Be nice," I whispered to him. "Hi, Mr. Baldwin," I said cheerfully with what I hoped would pass for a confident smile. "You'll never guess where Starling and I just were."

I looked around for Starling, who was slowly, reluctantly emerging from around his car.

"Am I to assume that this disgusting mop of a creature has something to do with it?" Mr. Baldwin said as I walked up to him.

I held out the puppy so that Mr. Baldwin

could see his face. I looked up hopefully, pray-
ing that the miraculous melting would occur
and that Mr. Baldwin would feel the same way
that I had the first time I had looked into those
eyes.

Well, forget that theory.

"I hate dogs," Mr. Baldwin announced.

"Now, Mr. Baldwin," Starling reasoned, finally catching up. "It isn't fair to judge all dogs
by what may have been a few negative
experiences."

"A *few*?" Mr. Baldwin roared, wheeling
around to go back inside. I followed, holding
the puppy tightly, with Starling behind me.
"When I was a mere lad, the neighbor's dog
knocked me in a mud puddle on the day that
the entire third grade was having its portrait
taken. I was a disgrace, and believe me, the
others never let me forget it."

"Well, that was just one bad experience," I
said optimistically. "Didn't you ever have a dog
of your own?"

"No, and I never wanted to," Mr. Baldwin
replied without a moment's hesitation. "They
smell, and they bark, and they lick themselves
in unseemly places. In fact, I've never had a
pet of any type. I despise those animal rights
people who claim that animals should never

suffer for the betterment of mankind. What drivel."

I looked at Starling, whose eyes were large behind his glasses. No, this wasn't exactly going well.

"Starling and I went to the SPCA today after school," I explained, finally deciding to leap in before Mr. Baldwin could expound any further on the worthlessness of animals.

"You certainly do know how to show a young lady a good time, Starling," Mr. Baldwin said sarcastically.

"Yes, I pride myself on the offbeat, the unusual. None of that predictable stuff like the mall," Starling said with a grin.

"And while we were there, I saw this puppy, and I absolutely couldn't leave it in that awful wire cage," I said, holding the puppy so that its face was toward Mr. Baldwin.

"Why ever not?" he asked.

"Well, after so many days or weeks, if the animals don't have homes, they have to kill them, and I just couldn't let that happen," I said, rushing through the words.

"So?" Mr. Baldwin said.

I looked desperately at Starling. This was it. "So I thought you might like him for company," I whispered.

"Bethany thought that you might enjoy having a dog," Starling echoed.

"Have you both taken leave of your senses?" Mr. Baldwin asked, looking from one of us to the other. "Have I by some horrible miscalculation of judgment said, done, or in any way given any intimation that I might want a dog?"

"No," I admitted.

"Good." Mr. Baldwin nodded. "I was afraid there for a moment that perhaps I really had lost my sanity. Now get that creature out of here."

"We can't," Starling said.

"Excuse me, young man, but the last time I checked the deed, this was my house, and as its owner I have the right to decide what does and does not live here."

"I just meant that we can't take it back to the SPCA today. They're closed."

I didn't know whether to thank Starling or hit him. He had gotten the puppy a temporary reprieve, but he had virtually promised to take it back tomorrow. I clutched the puppy tightly, stroking its spiky fur with a trembling hand. I couldn't imagine how I could stand to walk back into that SPCA and give back this puppy.

"Fine. Take it home with you, and dispose of it tomorrow." Mr. Baldwin was *very* serious.

"There's *one* problem there," Starling said.

"My mother is terribly allergic to dogs. Breaks out in hives and scratches until the blood flows at the mere sight of them."

"Then Miss Anderson will have to keep it overnight," Mr. Baldwin said firmly.

"I can't," I blurted out, my mind racing desperately.

"And why not, might I ask?"

My mind was completely and totally blank. It was like sitting down to take a test and having everything leave your mind. I couldn't think of even the most far-fetched of lies.

"Well, Miss Anderson?"

"Bethany *can't* take the puppy home," Starling said, looking at me hopefully.

"Why not?" Mr. Baldwin snapped.

"Well, it's a long story," Starling began.

I knew he was stalling, and I desperately tried to get my mind to function again, but I was sinking fast into verbal paralysis.

"Why don't you tell me the short version?" Mr. Baldwin said with a sigh.

"It has to do with her mother's death." Starling was on a roll.

I stared at him in amazement. He nodded at me. "Right, Bethany?"

I nodded.

Starling waited hopefully, but I added nothing to the storyline.

"Her mother had a dog that she was very fond of, and after her mother's death, Bethany's father found that dogs brought back very painful memories," Starling finished lamely.

I looked at Mr. Baldwin. I knew he wasn't buying this, but I could also see his hesitation to attack. He was probably ninety-nine percent certain that this was a bunch of bull, but that one percent risk that he was mocking my father's grief over my mother's death was holding him back.

"So we just need to leave it here until tomorrow. Then we'll take it back," Starling finished.

"What time does that animal place open?" Mr. Baldwin asked, sighing again.

"Probably in the morning, but we won't be able to go until after school," Starling said primly. "After all, we couldn't miss any of our classes."

Mr. Baldwin started to protest, but Starling had him there. No teacher — especially Mr. Baldwin — could justify our cutting class.

"I'll expect you the moment school dismisses for the day," Mr. Baldwin said.

"We'll be here," Starling promised. He went out on the porch and returned with the bag. "Here's everything he might need. We need to go now."

Mr. Baldwin raised one eyebrow. "Escaping, are you?"

"Homework, sir," Starling said very seriously. I nodded.

I had a nearly uncontrollable desire to race out of there with the puppy. How could I leave it with a man who obviously hated it? Still, it was better than the SPCA. Maybe I should take it home. Maybe I could convince my father that we needed a dog. I already knew what his answer would be. I would be going off to college in the fall, and he traveled a lot with his job. It wasn't fair to him or to the animal. Still, the puppy's contented little noises as he snuggled closer to me stole my heart.

"Give him the dog," Starling hissed. I broke out of my reverie. "Now," Starling said a little louder.

I still couldn't do anything. Starling pried the puppy out of my arms and handed him to Mr. Baldwin. Mr. Baldwin took him in outstretched hands as if he were receiving a package of meat dripping blood. "Can't he stand up?"

"Sure he can," Starling answered.

"Then he belongs on the floor." Mr. Baldwin put the puppy down, and the puppy promptly fell over.

"Pitiful," Mr. Baldwin said, shaking his head.

I started to bend down to help the puppy, but Starling grabbed my hand. "Better get going on our homework," he said while yanking me out of the door. "We'll see you tomorrow."

"You certainly will," Mr. Baldwin stated. "And don't for one instant believe that this transparent ploy is going to work and that I'm going to change my mind about keeping this beast. He goes back tomorrow."

"Yes, Mr. Baldwin," Starling conceded.

"I hate him," I said as soon as we were in the car, tears streaming down my face. "How can he not love that sweet little dog?"

"That's not fair," Starling said, starting the car and pulling away. "You're trying to impose your likes on him, and he's not buying it."

"But a dog would be good for him, and that puppy deserves a good home." My tears were falling faster.

"It won't work unless that's what Mr. Baldwin wants."

"And you said we'd take him back to the SPCA."

"What was I supposed to do? It *is* his house, and it *is* his life."

"But what about the puppy's life?"

"Bethany, let's worry about that tomorrow."

"I'm not going back tomorrow," I said, taking a deep breath and wiping my face.

Starling looked at me. "Oh, *yes*, you are."

"No, I'm not. Mr. Baldwin isn't allowed to drive yet, and if we don't go back, he'll have to keep the puppy."

"That isn't fair, and you know it."

"Fine, then, Starling, you go back."

"Bethany, I've been trying very hard not to say this, but you're pushing me too far. This was all your idea! You have to admit that, and you have to see it through."

I knew that none of this was Starling's fault, but that didn't help much. "You're cold-hearted, just like Mr. Baldwin," I shouted at him. "Neither of you has any compassion, any concern for anything other than yourself. I hope you're happy, because I'm sure not." By this time, we were in front of my house, and I threw open the car door and stormed away.

I thought Starling might come after me, but he drove away. Good, I thought. I can't stand any more of his logic. My father's car wasn't in the driveway, so I rummaged through my pocketbook for my keys.

That was when I saw them.

Three small red hearts were glued to the glass of the kitchen door.

I FEEL AS THOUGH I KNOW WHERE SHE
IS EVEN WHEN SHE IS NOT WITHIN
MY SIGHT. THERE IS A CONNECTION,
AN ENERGY CENTERED IN HER THAT
DRAWS ME TO HER, THAT ALLOWS
ME TO SENSE HER.

BETHANY.

HER NAME SUITS HER QUIET BEAUTY,
HER GENEROUS SPIRIT.

SHE IS THE ANSWER TO ALL THAT IS
MISSING WITHIN ME.

SHE IS THE PERFECTION THAT I SEEK.

SHE COULD NEVER DENY ME WHAT I
NEED TO LIVE.

Chapter 7

We have a clock that chimes on the hour and the half hour. I heard every one of those chimes that night. You name it, and I worried about it. All night.

First I fussed about Starling. Obviously he was playing games with those hearts. He had been at my house waiting for me, and he must have stuck them on the door to entertain himself while he was waiting — and, of course, to drive me crazy. I was mad at myself for buying his innocent act over the hearts on my locker. Why didn't he just admit that he'd had a whimsical moment and done something that was actually kind of sweet?

Of course, once I was done being annoyed with him, I could move on to full-fledged anger over his betrayal of the puppy. I mean, he'd probably condemned that animal to death by lethal injection or whatever it was that the

SPCA did. How could he not fight harder with Mr. Baldwin? Of course, I conveniently ignored the fact that I had been unable to speak during crucial parts of the argument.

Then I spent hours on Mr. Baldwin's senseless stubbornness. He had the perfect home to offer to that puppy, and the puppy would be good for him. Would he ever see that? If he ever saw it, would he ever admit it? Of course not!

What time remained I spent trying to decide if I should go to the University of Delaware and live at home so that I could launch a campaign to get my father to let me keep the dog. I mean, I'd already been accepted at the University, but I had also seriously considered living on campus. On the one hand, I wanted a taste of life away from home — or at least the few miles from my house to campus. On the other hand, I had a nice life worked out with my father. I guess my mother's death has brought us closer, and we've learned to cooperate while keeping out of each other's way. I'd have a lot more peace and quiet to study at home rather than in a dorm, but I'd miss out on that college life experience, whatever that was supposed to be.

Then there was Starling. He'd been accepted at the University of Delaware and every place else his parents had made him apply, including Princeton. His parents were pretty excited about the Ivy League, but Starling was putting off his decision. His theory was that he didn't really know what he wanted to do, so why spend that kind of money when he could explore his options at the University of Delaware for much less. Needless to say, Delaware's honors program was lusting after him, but Starling was missing deadline after deadline for making a commitment.

I didn't quite know how I felt about it. I would miss Starling terribly if he went away, but how many people get accepted at Princeton? Besides, our relationship wasn't a "certain we want to spend our lives together" kind of thing. Sometimes I didn't know if I wanted to spend the next five minutes with him.

I think I drifted off to sleep around three-thirty in the morning. I remember dreaming. In my dream, a pack of about thirty-five puppies was chasing Starling through Mr. Baldwin's house, and Mr. Baldwin was screaming that nobody respected the lessons of history.

The phone rang.

I got out of the bed and went to the phone in the hallway.

"Hello?" I said, waiting.

Silence.

"Hello?" I repeated, louder this time.

Silence.

There was complete silence, no line interference or distant signals, no breathing.

I was not having a good time, and this was all that I needed to make me mad — and a little frightened. "Hello?" I shouted. "Will you please say something?"

"Who is it?" I heard a sleepy voice say, and for a moment I thought it was the caller, but it was my father standing at his bedroom door.

I heard the dial tone click on.

"Nobody said anything," I said to my father.

"Jerk," my father said. Still, I thought I saw a glimmer of relief in his face, too.

All possibility of sleep was gone now. I considered doing some homework or reading, but I found myself much more preoccupied with worrying.

I wondered how the puppy was doing.

I wondered how Mr. Baldwin was doing.

I wondered if Starling was awake worrying, too.

Somehow I doubted it.

Chapter 8

I guess Starling took an educated guess and figured I wouldn't be in a very good mood the next morning. Considering how I'd shouted at him, I guess I'm lucky he was even speaking to me. As it was, he showed up at my house just as I was stumbling toward the refrigerator for my morning diet Pepsi.

I really don't see how people face orange juice at six-thirty.

"Good morning," Starling yelled through the kitchen door, banging on it enthusiastically.

Great, I thought. I haven't had any sleep, and the Good Humor man has come to visit.

"What?" I said, shoving my hair away from my face. Luckily we're not at the stage where I have to look absolutely perfect for him.

Actually, we've never been at that stage.

"I'm here to take you out to breakfast. How

about nice cholesterol-laden bacon and eggs to start the day?"

"You're sick. I hope you know that, Starling."

I cannot face anything more substantial than a doughnut in the morning, and Starling knows that.

"How about a cherry danish with a nice, refreshing glass of diet Pepsi on the side?"

There. That was better.

"I have to get dressed," I said.

"No," Starling said in sarcastic amazement. "You mean you're not ready to go off to school just as you are? I really have lost my fashion sense."

I had to smile. I was dressed in an extra-extra-large T-shirt of my father's that came to my knees, and bulky socks. Yes, yes, Bethany the fashion-conscious.

I bet Jyl *never*, ever looked like this. I bet she slept perfectly still on her back with her arms crossed on her chest so her perfect French braid never got disturbed. She could probably wear mascara to bed and wake up without a smudge. She could . . .

What was I doing? Nobody had even mentioned Jyl. I'm a scary creature on too little sleep.

"I'll be right back. The paper should be in

the driveway somewhere," I said to Starling as I headed toward the bathroom.

I heard him go back out the kitchen door, and when he came back in, the door slammed behind him. Great. Now he'd wake up my father for sure. I washed my face and got dressed as quickly as I could. Luckily, I'm fast. I bet it wasn't more than four minutes total.

I thought I'd come down to find Starling engrossed in the newspaper. Wrong. He looked decidedly unhappy.

Puppy? I thought hopefully. Does he feel bad about it now, too?

"Bethany, what are those hearts doing on your kitchen door?"

"Starling, I'm not in the mood for your games."

"No game, Bethany."

I looked at him carefully. True, he can fool me pretty easily, but I really studied his face and I could see no trace of his usual orneriness.

"I figured you put them there while you waited for me to get home from school yesterday," I said.

"Nope," Starling said. "I told you I didn't put those hearts on your locker, and I didn't have anything to do with these, either."

How strange. I walked over to the door and pulled it open, staring at the small constellation of three red hearts. There didn't seem to be anything out of the ordinary about them, except, of course, for the fact that they were on my door.

And on my locker.

"I don't like this," Starling said. "Anybody could know what locker you use at school, but who knows where you live?"

"Secret admirer?" I asked.

"Looks that way," Starling said.

I smiled at him. "Let's go," I said. "I'm hungry."

"That's it? That's all you have to say?" Starling said sharply.

"What would you like me to do?" I asked impatiently. "I don't think there's any law against little gummed red hearts. I doubt that putting them on the door constitutes assault or destruction of property or anything. Here. If they're bothering you, I'll scrape them off."

"Stop," Starling said, grabbing my hand.

"What? You don't want me to get rid of them? You want to stare at them some more?"

"Maybe they have drugs on them — or poison," Starling said seriously.

Now we were back on familiar ground. Starling and his bizarre theories.

I dragged him toward the driveway. "Right, Starling. Now fill me in on this. If there's anything unusual on those hearts, how is it supposed to be passed on since those hearts have already been licked? Drive while you answer that."

Starling headed the car toward Bing's Bakery on Main Street.

"Maybe it's a new kind of drug that will absorb through your skin if you touch the glue. Maybe it's activated by saliva, so that the next person who touches the surface is the one who gets the effect."

"Maybe some little kid got a sheet of hearts as a present or something and was going around the neighborhood sticking them places."

"And he also went to your locker at school? Don't you think that's a little farfetched, Bethany?"

"Okay, maybe it is, but your drug theory isn't exactly grounded in reality, either."

"Fine," Starling said. "So what's your reality-based theory?"

"I have a secret admirer," I said promptly, "and frankly I'm a little bit upset that you don't automatically accept that theory. Don't you think I'm capable of attracting someone's attention?"

Starling sidestepped that one pretty neatly. "Who do you think it is?"

I didn't want to give him the satisfaction of seeing me search my mind. "Rocco?" I suggested, giving him the first male I could think of.

Starling laughed loud and long.

"What?" I said. "Don't you think Rocco could be attracted to me?" I have to admit I had a smile on my face, too. When the ice storm trapped Starling and me and Mr. Baldwin in the school on the night that Mr. Baldwin had his heart attack, Rocco, along with Jyl and Herbert, was also there. He is a huge, musclebound, macho stud, and I say that affectionately. I like Rocco — much as you would like a Saint Bernard. He's big and not terribly dangerous, but you wouldn't want to push that theory too far.

"Can you see Rocco putting little red hearts on your locker and your door?" Starling asked, giving another loud snort of laughter.

"No," I admitted. "If he decided that he wanted someone, he'd be more likely to pick her up, throw her over his shoulder, and say something profound like, 'Yo, baby, how about you and me go mess around or something.' "

Starling nodded in agreement. "So who else? Herbert?"

"Starling!" I protested. Herbert was so timid and shy that I don't think he had ever approached a girl in his life. I hated to dismiss him so rapidly as a potential candidate for secret admirer, but Herbert with his plaids and pocket protectors just didn't fit the bill.

"So?" Starling said.

"So let's talk about the puppy," I said. This conversation was making me nervous.

"Let's not," Starling said.

"Why not?"

"It's a no-win situation. Anything I say, you'll end up calling me cold and heartless again."

"I didn't mean it, Starling," I said, taking a deep breath and knowing that I really did owe him an apology. "I was just upset."

"I know," he said. "It's just that we can't force an animal on Mr. Baldwin, and neither of us can keep the puppy."

"That's it! Maybe we can find someone else to take him."

"Who?" Starling said.

"Rocco?" I suggested.

"He'd probably bench press it to death," Starling said. "Besides, I don't think a scrawny little thing like that would fit his image."

"He's not scrawny," I protested. "He's just not filled in yet."

"Herbert?" Starling suggested. "They'd look good together."

"Stop insulting the puppy," I said before I realized how that reflected on poor Herbert. "That's a possibility." Then I came up with another idea. I didn't like it one little bit, but I liked the thought of taking the dog back to the SPCA even less. "How about Jyl?" I suggested. "I'm sure that if *you* suggested it to her, she'd not only take the dog but she'd buy it designer outfits and let it sleep with her at night."

"Bethany, you never let up on Jyl, do you? Okay, I'll ask her and you ask Herbert."

It wasn't much of a plan, but it would have to do.

A cherry danish and a few minutes later, we walked into school. "Maybe the puppy is growing on Mr. Baldwin," I suggested hopefully before Starling and I went our separate ways to homeroom.

Right.

IT IS TIME.

I WILL BE CAREFUL.

I WILL NOT STARTLE HER.

I WILL DO NOTHING THAT MIGHT MAKE
HER TAKE HER BEAUTY AND GRACE
AWAY FROM ME.

BUT I NEED TO SEE HER.

I NEED TO HEAR THE SOUND OF HER
VOICE AGAIN.

I NEED TO MAKE HER UNDERSTAND
THAT SHE IS MINE IN EVERY WAY.

Chapter 9

-

Herbert sneezes nonstop in the presence of dogs. He claims that dogs have dandruff that makes his throat spasm.

Jyl said that if it was really important to Starling, she'd call Swarthmore College and beg them to bend the rules just a little teeny bit for her so she could take the puppy to school with her next year. She said that if the puppy was half as cute as Starling, then she knew she'd love it at first sight.

Of course, that's Starling's version, and there was an evil glint in his eyes as he told me this. I think it might be another Starling Horace Whitman the Fifth ploy to get my attention.

As if he doesn't have it already.

I suffered through the day, trying to focus on my classes but really just counting down the hours until we had to go to Mr. Baldwin's and get the puppy.

Starling said he'd meet me at my locker at the end of the day. I think he knew that if he gave me any chance, I'd bolt and he'd have to go to Mr. Baldwin's by himself. He was right.

I walked as slowly as I could down the noisy hallway as 1400 students emptied the building. Sure enough, there was Starling, leaning against my locker. I didn't say anything and he moved aside so I could unlock the combination and throw my books in. Somehow I didn't think I'd be in much of a mood to do homework.

I rotated the knob of the lock almost by feel, barely needing to look at the numbers. I yanked open the door, then lifted the lever that released the smaller door of the top section. I almost had let go of my books to throw them in when I saw something in the top section of the locker.

I looked at Starling, who was nonchalantly leaning against the next locker, and smiled as I took out a single red rose. It was stuck into one of those little vials of water with the plastic top, and the rose was fresh and beautiful, the bud just beginning to open.

"Starling," I said. "You shouldn't have."

He turned to face me, and his eyes locked

on the rose. "Bethany, I didn't," he said. He practically lunged for the rose, taking it out of my hand.

Tied around the stem was a ribbon, and dangling from the ribbon was a small envelope like florists use. This one, however, had no flower shop name on it. Lettered in neat block letters, however, was BETHANY.

"Don't you dare," I said, grabbing the rose back before Starling could open the envelope.

I finished getting rid of my books, shut my locker, and began to walk down the hallway.

"Aren't you even curious?" Starling said, coming after me.

Curious? I was dying. Still, I had a perverse desire to make Starling suffer.

It didn't take long, though, before I couldn't stand it. I carefully opened the envelope and took out the small card. The same neat block lettering covered the front. Starling was peering over my shoulder as I read:

I ONLY WISH THERE WERE A FLOWER MORE LOVELY,
ONE THAT COULD DESERVE TO COME CLOSE TO YOU.

That was it. No name, nothing. Starling ripped the card out of my hand and flipped it over, but all he found was the blank back.

"So whose handwriting is this?" he asked.

"Beats me. Rocco?" I suggested to break the tension.

"Be serious."

"Seriously, I don't know. Don't worry about it."

"Don't worry about it? Somebody thinks you're more lovely than a rose."

"And you don't?"

"And somebody knows your locker combination," Starling added quickly. "And that leaves me out."

I hadn't thought about that. Even Starling didn't know my locker combination. There simply had never been a need to tell him what it was, and I'd never told anyone else, either.

"Maybe somebody in the office told someone," I said vaguely. "I'll ask tomorrow."

"Do that," Starling said.

I have to admit that I was enjoying this. Before Starling, nobody had ever paid much attention to me. After all, that was the way I wanted it. My father's military career had made me an expert at changing schools — seventeen times at last count — and I had learned early to keep a distance from people I'd probably be leaving in a few months. My father's retirement from the Army had changed that — and so had Starling. No matter how much grief I gave him, he still came back.

Still, the idea of somebody lusting after me from afar was flattering and fun. If it made Starling sweat a little, all the better.

Besides, we were almost to Mr. Baldwin's house before I started to get upset about the puppy, so the rose was good for something.

"Be calm," Starling said. "We did our best."

"I know," I said, but I could already feel the start of tears behind my eyes.

We walked up to Mr. Baldwin's door. He wasn't standing there waiting for us, but the door was open. We knocked and called in to him, then went in the screen door.

Imagine our surprise.

There was a woman in Mr. Baldwin's living room.

And that woman was holding the puppy.

"Hello, Mr. Baldwin," we both said.

"It's about time," Mr. Baldwin snapped.

We waited for him to introduce his guest, but he didn't. She seemed to be about sixty-five or so with gray, short-cropped hair and bright blue eyes. She had a big smile on her face as she talked to the puppy.

"Aren't you the best little snookums in the world?" she cooed. "Aren't you just the sweetest little snookums that ever breathed?"

Mr. Baldwin began to pace back and forth. I worried briefly about his heart. Starling was looking around with a confused look on his face.

"I was taking the beast for a walk so that it could take care of its necessary functions," Mr. Baldwin began.

"And he just didn't know the first thing about taking a sweet little thing like this for a walk," the woman interrupted.

I waited for Mr. Baldwin's explosion, but he seemed to be huffing too loudly for words.

"Why, the poor thing was about to choke," the woman continued. "And Seth here was just tugging on the leash like this was a rhinoceros or a wildebeest or something instead of a sweet little snookums."

Seth?

"The sweet little snookums was lying down in the middle of the street refusing to walk," Mr. Baldwin finally snapped. His voice dripped with sarcasm.

"And Seth was yelling at him, as if that was going to help," the woman continued. " 'Beast, get up on your feet and walk, you incorrigible mop of flesh and fur,' " the woman bellowed in an excellent imitation of Mr. Baldwin. Starling and I looked at each other and barely suppressed a laugh.

"What was I supposed to do, let the approaching car run over us both?" Mr. Baldwin asked.

"So here he is, dragging this poor baby along," the woman said, voice filled with outrage.

"It was perfectly capable of walking," Mr. Baldwin said.

"Not after you'd terrorized it," the woman said. "So I just swooped it up and came home to give this man some lessons on how to train a dog to walk on a leash."

Somebody give Mr. Baldwin lessons? This should be good.

"Quite unnecessary," Mr. Baldwin snapped. "These young people are here to take that animal back to the SPCA where they mistakenly got it."

"No!" the woman screamed. "You may *not* do that. I won't let you."

"And who, might I ask, are you to tell me what I may and may not do?" Mr. Baldwin yelled. If I'd been that woman, I would have been quivering in my shoes. She, however, seemed totally unimpressed.

"I'm Anna," she said calmly. "Anna Winters. I already told you that. Don't you remember?" She smiled at Mr. Baldwin.

"I'm Starling. Pleased to meet you." Starling

held out his hand, and Anna extricated one hand from around the puppy and shook it.

"Bethany Anderson," I said. Her hand was warm, her handshake firm.

"Pleased to meet you both," she said. "Seth didn't tell me he had grandchildren."

"They are not related," Mr. Baldwin said quickly. "They are former students of mine."

"We're his friends," I said, unwilling to be relegated to just former student status.

"Good for you," Anna said with a smile. "I'm sure it's not easy."

This time Starling didn't manage to stifle his laugh. He tried to cover it with a cough, but it was pretty clear what he'd been doing. Mr. Baldwin looked like he was ready to explode.

"What time do you get up in the morning?" Anna asked Mr. Baldwin.

"I don't see where that is of any concern to you," Mr. Baldwin said sharply.

"Just answer the question," Anna said.

"Approximately seven A.M.," Mr. Baldwin answered, much to my amazement.

"We'll walk at eight. Be ready on time," Anna said.

"There will be no animal here to walk," Mr. Baldwin said, his face turning red.

"Of course there will be," Anna said. The puppy raised his head and looked around sleepily. I went over to him and scratched between his ears. He stretched out on Anna's lap in contentment.

"We need to go," Starling said, bending down to pet the dog. "You remember."

"Oh, yes, that meeting where . . ."

"My father is being honored for the many contributions he has made to . . ."

" . . . last quarter's profit margin," I finished. "Of course. How could I have forgotten. See you later, Mr. Baldwin."

We were almost to the door before Mr. Baldwin bellowed. "You two are not going anywhere," he said, his voice deep and authoritative. "You are going to get rid of this beast, and you are going to do it now."

"Oh, shut up, Seth. Let those children alone," we heard Anna say as we dashed out the door and down the driveway. We must have set speed records for getting in the car, getting it started, and driving away.

"That woman told Mr. Baldwin to shut up," Starling said in amazement.

"Do you think she's still alive?" I asked, shaking my head.

"Do you want to go back and find out?" Starling asked.

"No way. Besides, we have to go to that dinner, remember?"

"At least you helped me lie — er — exaggerate this time," Starling said.

"At least the puppy gets to stay for another day," I said. I picked the rose up from where I had laid it on the dash of the car. I read the note one more time.

Who could it possibly be from?

"Stop mooning over that stupid flower," Starling said.

"Shut up," I said sweetly.

"What?" Starling said. "Are there uppity women everywhere these days?"

"You better believe it," I said.

"Poor men. We just don't stand a chance," Starling said with a sigh.

"Now you're learning," I said with a smile.

I THINK OF HER MORE AND MORE.

AND WITH THOSE THOUGHTS COME
    THE NEED TO HEAR HER VOICE.
SHE DESERVES THE MOON AND THE
    SKY AND THE STARS.
SHE DESERVES TO BE TREATED WITH
    PERFECT CONSIDERATION.
SHE DESERVES TO KNOW HOW SPECIAL
    SHE IS, TO BE WOOED AND HONORED
    WITH THE PUREST LOVE.
SHE DESERVES MY HEART.

BETHANY.

SHE WILL BE MINE.

Chapter 10

"How many people are in the senior class?" Starling asked the next day as we were on our way to Mr. Baldwin's. I have to admit that at least a tiny bit of optimism lurked in my mind; after all, the puppy had had another twenty-four hours to win Mr. Baldwin over, thanks to Anna.

"Well?" Starling said.

"I don't know," I said. I mean, I go to the school, but I don't keep much of an inventory of who's there.

"Humor me and take a guess," Starling said.

"Okay, divide 1400 by four," I said, remembering the total enrollment.

"Three hundred and fifty," Starling said. Jyl didn't call him Einstein for nothing. "Yes, but don't a lot of people drop out before their senior year?"

"I suppose, Starling," I said, my mind on the puppy.

"So let's say that actually the senior class only has about three hundred people."

"Fine, Starling. What is this, census year or something?"

"And how many relatives and friends would you say that each of those seniors has?"

"How am I supposed to know something like that?" I said impatiently.

"How many do you have?" Starling said.

"I have my father, an aunt in another state, you, and maybe Rocco and Herbert." This was depressing. It wasn't a very big collection of family and friends.

"Five," Starling said. "So let's at least double that for most people."

"Thanks a lot, Starling," I said. "Mr. Diplomacy strikes again."

"Sorry, Beach. I didn't mean it to sound that way."

"Is it my fault that I don't have many relatives?" I said. It probably was my fault that I didn't have many friends, but I didn't want to discuss that. "Wait — Mr. Baldwin. Add him to my list."

"Six times two is twelve, times three hundred is thirty-six hundred. Wow," Starling marveled. "That's a lot of people."

"Starling, are you going to dazzle me with math, or are you going to tell me what you're mumbling about?"

"I got called into the principal's office right at the end of seventh period," Starling said, as if that explained everything.

"Oh, no. What have you done this time?" I asked. The worry had already started flooding my mind.

"I am highly insulted," Starling said with a huff. "Besides, you sound exactly like my mother."

"Starling, what have you done?" He couldn't pull off an innocent act with me. Starling isn't exactly evil, but he certainly does have an ornery streak. He blames it on boredom. School is really easy for him, thanks in part to his photographic memory, so he seeks diversions to entertain himself. Let's just say that some bizarre occurrences have resulted.

"I was called in to be praised, not punished," Starling said in a lofty voice.

"Sure," I said sarcastically.

"You really shouldn't scoff at me," Starling said. "After all, you are looking at the valedictorian of the senior class."

"No," I said without thinking. Then I stopped to consider the facts. Ever since I'd known Starling, which was almost two years now, he'd gotten nothing but A's. I guess it was reasonable to suppose that the first two years had been the same.

"Do you have a 4.0 grade point average?" I asked.

"Of course," he said, with no false modesty.

"And you really are the valedictorian?" I asked.

"You know, I had the distinct impression that the principal was not especially thrilled over it," Starling said with a laugh. "After all, I'm not exactly his favorite person, but valedictorian is based strictly on grades, and I'm the only one with a 4.0."

"Who's next?" I asked out of curiosity.

"Jyl," Starling said. "Actually, the principal spent a great deal of time telling me about how Jyl is Honor Society president, senior class secretary, and a wonderful representative of our school."

"That jerk!" I exploded. "He was trying to get you to decline being valedictorian and turn it over to her."

"You're right," Starling said.

I wheeled on him, grabbing his face and turning it so that I could see his eyes. Luckily we were stopped at a red light at the time. "You didn't. Starling, tell me you didn't."

"Why would you care? You laughed at the

idea of my being valedictorian. Why shouldn't I give the honor to somebody who deserves it?"

"Starling, you didn't. Not Jyl."

"Ah-ha!" Starling said. "It's not that you want to hear a memorable, inspiring speech from me on graduation night; you just don't want me to do something nice for Jyl."

The car behind us honked impatiently. I almost turned around and gave the driver the finger before I realized that I had never given anybody the finger in my whole life and this probably wasn't a good time to start. I'd just keep both hands free to strangle Starling.

"Starling, this isn't funny. Answer me."

"I told the principal I'd think about it and let him know," Starling said.

"You're giving that speech," I said firmly.

"Why?" Starling said.

"Because it would make your parents happy," I said, searching desperately for reasons that had nothing to do with Jyl.

"That depends on what I said," Starling responded, wiggling his eyebrows. That expression gave me a new direction of worry.

"Starling, would you really give some off-the-wall graduation speech?" I asked. I don't know why I bothered, I already knew the answer.

"Graduation speeches tend to be so boring," Starling said. "You know, all those 'Tonight is not an end, but a beginning,' speeches. Those 'We are trees, our roots nourished by our families, our branches reaching out to the sun' speeches. I really don't think I could stand to give one of those."

"You could give a great speech, Starling, without being too . . ."

"Bizarre?" he suggested.

"Right," I said.

"Tell you what," Starling said. "I'll write a speech, and I'll let you decide whether I should give that speech or turn it over to Jyl. Remember, at least 3600 people will hear it. The decision is yours."

"Starling, you can't do that to me."

"Fine. I'll tell the principal that I don't want to be valedictorian."

"Write," I said. I vowed that unless the speech was absolutely going to kill his parents or create a legacy that would come back to haunt him, I'd tell Starling to give it.

Jyl? No way.

We were at Mr. Baldwin's before I realized that I'd forgotten to worry about the puppy. We went to the door and knocked. There was no answer. I put my hand on the doorknob, ready to see if the door was unlocked, when Starling stopped me.

"You'd better not," he said. "You might be interrupting something."

"What?" I asked, confused.

"You know, Anna and Mr. Baldwin might be . . ." Starling gave me a wink.

I looked at him in amazement. "Starling, how could you ever think that?"

"Are you implying that Mr. Baldwin couldn't . . ."

Luckily, before Starling could finish his statement, I heard Mr. Baldwin's voice. "Well, come in here. Don't just stand there rattling the doorknob."

I smiled smugly at Starling.

We walked into the living room, and what I saw brought a huge smile to my face. Mr. Baldwin was sitting on the sofa, and curled up next to him with his head on Mr. Baldwin's leg was the puppy.

"Stupid beast won't leave me in peace," Mr. Baldwin said, but there was something that didn't quite ring true about his snarl.

"How was your lesson with Anna?" Starling said innocently.

"I didn't go," Mr. Baldwin said sharply.

"Why not?" I asked.

"I didn't want to," he answered simply.

"Didn't she come to get you?" I asked. Somehow Anna had struck me as a rather determined lady.

"Certainly," Mr. Baldwin said. "I refused to answer the door."

"Mr. Baldwin, what if she's worried about you? What if she thinks something happened to you?" I said.

"Let her worry," Mr. Baldwin said, his old fire returning to his eyes. "I never asked her to take an interest in me or my . . ." He caught himself. "Or in this incorrigible beast."

The incorrigible beast stirred in his sleep. The puppy opened one tired eye, looked up at Mr. Baldwin, then settled back on Mr. Baldwin's leg. Mr. Baldwin's hand actually started toward the puppy's head, but he stopped himself.

I'd say the puppy was leading in this round.

"Does this mean that the dog hasn't been walked all day?" Starling asked. "Bethany and I will take him out now if you want."

I held my breath, still afraid that Mr. Baldwin would tell us to keep going with the dog, right back to the SPCA.

"Of *course* I took him out," Mr. Baldwin replied. "I just waited until that infernal woman stopped banging on my door."

"Did he do any better at walking?" I asked cautiously.

"Of course he did," Mr. Baldwin said. "I certainly do not need some officious pseudo-dog expert to show me how to keep a four-legged beast moving along."

"Good," Starling said. "Glad to hear it. How about if we make you some dinner?"

"I'm perfectly capable of doing that myself," Mr. Baldwin said. "After all, you've made such precipitous exits the last two days that I have had to fend for myself whether I wanted to or not."

"Sorry," I said, realizing that I'd been so worried about the puppy that I'd forgotten about Mr. Baldwin's dinners. "Do you need anything from the store?"

"We'll scout around," Starling said.

"Turn on the television," Mr. Baldwin said. "The news should be on."

"The remote control is right over there," Starling said, but I jabbed him in the ribs with my elbow. I grabbed the remote, switched on the television, and put the remote on the sofa right next to Mr. Baldwin.

In the kitchen, Starling rubbed his ribs. "What was that for?" he said.

"Can't you see? Mr. Baldwin didn't want to disturb the puppy," I said. "The puppy's winning. Isn't this great?"

Suddenly I heard a bellow from the living

room. "What is the meaning of this?!"

I dashed to the living room to find Mr. Baldwin catapulting himself off the sofa, holding the puppy out in front of him. I looked at the sofa with dread. Sure enough, there was a wet spot.

Starling grabbed the puppy from Mr. Baldwin. "I'll take him out," he said. Then he smiled sweetly at me. "Bethany will scrub off your sofa," he said, making a hasty exit before I could complain.

Starling didn't even have to say it. I could read his mind. *This was all your idea, Bethany.*

Mr. Baldwin was looking at his sofa in horror.

"Don't worry," I said. "Some soap and water, and it'll be as good as new."

"That dreadful beast urinated on my furniture," he said.

"Puppies are like that," I said reassuringly. "They sleep so soundly that sometimes they forget what they're doing."

"That's why they should live in cages at the SPCA," Mr. Baldwin said, a scowl on his face.

I dashed for paper towels, wetting them and adding soap. I scrubbed frantically at the sofa, making what looked like a bigger mess as the wet area spread.

"It's just a brief stage," I said. "He really didn't mean any harm."

"Tell that to my sofa," Mr. Baldwin said.

"Why don't you just sit there in the chair and watch the news, and I'll have this as good as new in a moment," I said frantically.

Mr. Baldwin huffed as he settled in his chair. I hoped that there was something on the news that would capture his attention — a murder, arson, war.

I stared at the huge wet spot on the sofa, wondering if Mr. Baldwin had a blow dryer that I could use to help dry it. Somehow I doubted it. I blotted up the moisture as best I could, then retreated to the kitchen where I began to assemble the ingredients for a chicken-and-rice casserole. Mr. Baldwin's grumblings eventually quieted down.

I had the casserole half made when Mr. Baldwin appeared at the kitchen doorway. "Where are they?" he asked.

"What?"

"The beast and its keeper," Mr. Baldwin snapped.

"I don't know," I said. "Want me to go look for them?"

"He's probably lost the creature, or else he's lying down in the middle of the road somewhere."

I wanted to ask if he meant Starling or the puppy, but I bit my tongue. "I'm sure they're both fine," I said. "Starling's very good with dogs." I don't quite know why I said that since I've never seen Starling with any kind of dog before, except this puppy, which tended to growl at him.

"I'm glad I'm surrounded by such a group of experts," Mr. Baldwin grumbled.

With that, there was a knock at the door.

"See. There they are." Why was Starling knocking?

I heard the door open, and then I heard a voice that definitely wasn't Starling's. "Seth? Seth? Are you here? And where is that darling little snookums?"

"I'll go find Starling," I told Mr. Baldwin, who was looking out toward the living room with a stricken expression on his face.

"Don't you dare leave me alone with that woman." There was actually a pleading tone in his voice. I certainly had never heard *that* from Mr. Baldwin before.

"If I stay, will you keep the puppy?" I whispered. I knew it was a low blow, but I was desperate.

Mr. Baldwin didn't have a chance to reply before Anna descended upon us.

Chapter 11

Starling and "the beast" returned right after Anna's arrival, much to my relief, and Starling promptly invited Anna to stay for dinner. Mr. Baldwin looked about ready to kill Starling, but Anna swooped him away to the living room to talk about how to walk a puppy and to tell him how worried she was when he didn't answer the door that morning, and just where was he, anyway.

The woman was a human whirlwind, and Starling and I retreated to the kitchen to finish dinner and recover.

I was tearing up lettuce for a salad when Starling attacked me, grabbing me and dipping me backwards and kissing me.

"What was that for?" I asked once I could breathe again.

"It's all the passion in the air," Starling said, looking toward the living room. "We can't let the older generation get ahead of us."

"Starling, I don't think that Mr. Baldwin and Anna are out there in the living room making out on the sofa."

"How do you know?"

"Well, to begin with, Anna hasn't stopped talking," I reminded him.

"Listen — " Starling started. But at the moment, all I could hear was the newscaster.

"See? I'm right," Starling said, hugging me.

"Go check," I said. "Whatever Mr. Baldwin is doing with Anna, you can come back and do with me." Somehow I felt safe making that deal.

Starling crept toward the kitchen door and disappeared. He was back in a matter of seconds. "Rip off all your clothes and hit the floor," he said, racing into the kitchen as he began to unbutton his shirt.

"Starling!"

"A deal's a deal," he said, reaching for the button on his jeans.

"*Starling!*" I hissed. That's when I heard Anna's voice. Before Starling could strip any further, she was at the kitchen door.

"Is there anything I can help you children with?" Anna said, fully clothed.

"No, we're perfectly capable of doing it on our own," Starling replied, looking at me.

"Starling!" I said for the third time, hoping Anna didn't have a clue. "We're fine," I said to her.

"Speak for yourself," Starling whispered, moving behind Anna and buttoning buttons with a surly look on his face. I smiled at him.

Anna was starting to look decidedly confused.

"Maybe you could keep Mr. Baldwin company?" I suggested.

"Okay," she said, turning to go. She certainly must be a glutton for punishment.

"Do you think he's starting to like the puppy?" I asked before she went.

"Of course he is." Anna smiled. "Who couldn't love such a sweet little snookums?"

"Mr. Baldwin," Starling and I answered — but Anna was gone.

"I wish you'd stop trying to seduce me right here in Mr. Baldwin's kitchen," Starling said, making a big show of keeping his distance from me.

"I know," I sighed. "It's just that I have this thing for valedictorians."

"Ah-ha," Starling said, a little too loudly. "And here I thought it was my body."

"That, too," I sighed again. "Here. Cut up this tomato."

Starling flexed his muscles and went into a

samurai warrior stance. He massacred the tomato, but at least his mind was off sex for a while.

At least I guess it was. With Starling, it's hard to tell.

Over dinner we learned that Anna's husband had died of cancer three years ago, that she lived four blocks away from Mr. Baldwin, that she used to be a secretary for one of the big DuPont company executives but that she retired when her husband became ill, and that she walked every day.

"Mr. Baldwin's doctors have recommended that he walk, too," I said helpfully.

"Great form of exercise," Anna added. "Of course, I'm a rather enthusiastic walker. I doubt if Seth could keep up with me."

"I believe that I could keep up with the walker of my choice if I so desired," Mr. Baldwin huffed.

"He should start out slowly and build up time and distance," I added quickly, afraid that Mr. Baldwin's stubbornness would have him out walking ten miles the first day.

"I could stop near the end of my walk and pick you up," Anna suggested.

"I don't believe that will be necessary," Mr. Baldwin said shortly. I could have kicked him.

"Fine. Then I'll stop and pick up your dog.

At least somebody in this household should lead a healthy life," Anna retorted.

Starling and I looked at each other in amazement. This lady simply didn't take offense.

I liked her. A lot. I just wished that Mr. Baldwin would be nicer to her.

Starling and I did the dishes, and Anna said that she was expecting a call from her daughter in Arizona and left. Mr. Baldwin and the puppy watched a special on World War II.

"You know, it wouldn't kill you to walk with Anna." It couldn't hurt to try.

"It also wouldn't kill me to put bamboo spikes under my fingernails or vote for a Democrat, but I don't plan to do either," Mr. Baldwin retorted.

I was afraid to push him any further, so Starling and I made a hasty exit.

"Do you think the danger period is over for the puppy?" I asked Starling as we drove to my house.

"With a normal person, yes," Starling said. "With Mr. Baldwin, that puppy could be at risk of eviction for the rest of its life."

When we pulled up to my house, Starling and I both noticed something missing: my father's car.

"Is your dad working late?" Starling asked, a hopeful note in his voice.

"Not that I know." I headed up the driveway to the kitchen door. The three red hearts were still there. I was going to have to remember to take them off before my father started asking questions I couldn't answer.

We went into the house, and on the refrigerator was a note from my father.

Bethany —
Emergency trip to California — just found out, airport shuttle picks me up in five minutes. Sorry I couldn't see you before I left. I'll call when I get there.

— Dad
— Look in the living room. They were at the door when I went to leave. Starling?

I looked up from the note, which, of course, Starling was reading over my shoulder. What did my father think Starling had done?

Starling was already headed for the living room before I could catch up with him. We both stopped short, staring at the coffee table in front of the sofa.

There, stuck in a vase, were a dozen red roses.

"Starling?" I asked tentatively, already knowing the answer.

"Nope."

There was a card stuck in among the flowers, and I opened the envelope.

This time there were no words, just red hearts. In fact, both the front and back were nearly covered with those red gummed hearts.

"Do you know how much a dozen roses costs?" Starling finally said.

"No," I said, my mind racing.

"A lot."

I couldn't even make a joke about it. This was getting a little weird. I stared at the hearts, waiting for an inspiration that would solve this confusion.

No inspiration struck.

"Your secret admirer sure has expensive taste," Starling said.

"That leaves out most of the people I know," I said.

"So rub it in that I don't have enough money to buy you roses," Starling said.

"That's not what I meant and you know it," I said. I picked up the vase and took the flowers into the kitchen. I knew that it would make Starling feel better if I threw them away, but I just couldn't bring myself to do it. They were a beautiful, deep red with a rich, fresh smell.

I settled for putting them out of sight.

Starling was stretched out on the sofa when

I got back from the kitchen. I sat down on the floor beside him.

"Your father's gone," Starling said wistfully. "Far, far away. On the whole other side of the country."

"And he trusts me to behave while he's gone," I said. My father's trust was very important to me. He worried about me a lot, but he also trusted that I wouldn't let him down. In his own way, he also trusted Starling. I knew that my father didn't like Starling being here when he was away, but he also knew that he couldn't stop us from spending time together.

In fact, my dad spent a certain amount of time being tough around Starling just to remind him that he was a career military officer who was capable of killing, maiming, or doing whatever else was necessary to get the job done, but he actually liked Starling a lot.

He just didn't want me to have sex with him.

I agreed. I wasn't ready for that kind of commitment, and I wasn't ready for all the risk that went along with it. But Starling made that a little difficult to remember at times.

Still, one of the things that I liked about Starling was his ability to take "no" as the final word.

Actually, I have a theory about Starling. I don't think he's ready to have sex, either, and he feels safe in teasing me about it because he *knows* that I'll say no. If I actually said yes, he'd probably get totally flustered and run.

That's my theory, but I'm not willing to test it.

Starling left a few hours later. I walked him to the door, not wanting him to leave but knowing that he should. He stepped out into the warm spring air but then stopped suddenly.

"What's this?"

He was staring at the glass pane of the kitchen door.

"It's those stupid hearts," I said, not wanting to get into it again.

"How many were there?" he asked.

I stepped out to look at the door. Four hearts. I looked at them carefully.

"Weren't there three before?" Starling asked.

"There might have been four," I said, but I could have sworn there were only three. I racked my brain, trying to recreate the image of the hearts when we came in the door a few hours before.

Three? I thought so, but I couldn't be sure.

Suddenly I reached up and scraped all the hearts off with my thumbnail. "There. No hearts," I said.

Starling still looked worried. "Do you think this heart person came back?" he said.

"Of course not," I said. "Or if he did, it was probably when he brought the flowers."

"Right," Starling said. "Are you sure that you want me to leave?"

"Of course," I said with conviction I didn't really feel. Still, I was not going to be unnerved by some silly little hearts. Somebody had a crush on me and put hearts around and sent me flowers. How dangerous could that be? I didn't need anybody worrying about me, not even Starling. I was perfectly capable of taking care of myself.

At least that's what I told Starling. Still, I was careful to lock the door behind him, and I double-checked the front door and the windows. My bedroom window was open a few inches, and I shut it, even though my room was on the second floor and the evening was warm.

I could have sworn that there were only three hearts on the door when I came home.

Had the person been back while Starling and I were there?

Had he seen us?

I checked downstairs again. The curtains had been drawn in the living room, but they didn't exactly meet in the middle. There was definitely still a narrow opening.

Had someone been watching?

Had he wanted me to know that he was there?

Stop it, I said to myself. You're being ridiculous.

I almost had myself convinced by the time I finally fell asleep, hours later after listening for every little sound.

Normally, it doesn't bother me at all when my father is away on business. In fact, I kind of enjoy the privacy.

Tonight, California seemed very far away.

I fell asleep counting roses and red hearts.

IT IS NOT HER FAULT.

IT IS SIMPLY THAT SHE DOESN'T KNOW ME YET.
ONCE SHE REALIZES THAT SHE IS PERFECT FOR ME AND THAT I AM DEVOTED TO MAKING HER HAPPY, SHE WILL KNOW THAT THERE IS ONLY ONE PATH TO FOLLOW.

SHE WILL BE WITH ME, ONLY ME.

I MUST MAKE HER REALIZE THAT LIFE IS WASTED UNTIL WE ARE TOGETHER.

I MUST LET HER KNOW WHO I AM.

Chapter 12

I had gone to see her the minute I got to school the next morning.

"What is so important about a locker combination?" the secretary in the attendance office asked.

"Well, you see, Mrs. List, someone left something in my locker, and I'd like to know how he managed to do that," I said politely.

"Was it something dangerous? A bomb? Something threatening?" Mrs. List asked, her attractive face concerned.

"Actually, it was a rose," I admitted.

"And you're complaining? You should be thanking whoever gave him the combination." Mrs. List turned back to her work with a smile.

"Are you saying that you gave out my combination?" I asked.

"No," Mrs. List answered. "Although I have to admit that if a young man showed up with roses, I might be tempted. How romantic."

"How else could somebody get into it?" I asked, more to myself than to her.

"The custodians have master keys," Mrs. List said. "But I wouldn't worry about it too much. If he's interested enough in you to give you roses, he'll make himself known before those roses fade. He'll want to take credit for them. Wait. Here comes Mrs. Dawson. Why don't you ask her? She's sometimes kind of psychic about things, especially when it comes to romance."

Feeling stupid, I explained the situation to Mrs. Dawson. She tried her best, but she had neither information nor intuition to help me.

I thanked them both and left. Mrs. List was right. As Starling had mentioned, roses were expensive. Somebody wouldn't give me a dozen and then not even give me a chance to thank him.

Would he?

I hurried to physics and sat next to Starling. For once, Jyl was in her own seat.

"Did you find out who has locker combinations?" he asked as soon as I came in.

"Mrs. List," I said, "but she says she didn't give mine out."

"Who else?"

"Custodians have a master key. Mrs. List said that whoever gave me the flowers will show up for the gratitude," I said, pulling out my notebook and getting ready for class.

"And how grateful are you?" Starling asked.

"Grateful enough to throw myself at his feet and beg him to do unspeakable things to my body," I said with a smile.

Starling promptly pulled out his wallet and all the change in his pocket. "How many roses do you think I could buy with $4.92?" he asked.

"Not enough." I was still smiling.

"Maybe I could sell my body on the street corner," he said.

"I thought you wanted to *make* money," I said, turning my attention to the teacher.

I concentrated on class, pushing away thoughts of roses and Starling. I mean, I get A's in the class, but I work for them. Starling, on the other hand, spent the period writing. At the end of class, he shoved several sheets of paper at me.

"Here. Read this and let me know what you think," he said, getting up to leave. I took the sheets and started after him, then realized that he'd already been intercepted by Jyl. I read as I walked to my next class.

Valedictory Speech, Draft One

Tonight, on this (choose one of the following: hot, warm, cool, breezy, stagnant, suffocating, rainy, humid with a thirty percent chance of thunderstorms) evening, we come together for one last time as a class.

For this I say halleluyah (Hallelujah? hallelooyehah? Oh forget it, this is a speech.). Never have I been more ready to leave behind an institution than I am this one.

I groaned.

Where else could you find people enthusiastically supporting the legal battering of fellow human beings by means of head-banging, bone-crushing, injury-intending behavior embellished by cursing and spitting, and not only allow this to happen but sell tickets and call it a sport?

Okay, okay, I thought, so you don't like football, Starling. This is going to win you fans right off the bat for this speech. I could see the football team rising out of their seats and storming the podium. Great move, Starling.

Where else could you find young males grasping and holding other young males in bizarre

*locations with questionable intent, and sell tick-
ets to that, also?*

I didn't realize that Starling felt so strongly
about wrestling, too.

*Where else can you find underpaid adults
being reduced to the role of baby-sitter, amateur
psychiatrist, mother, father, nursemaid, house-
keeper, butler, and prison warden in order to
attempt to smash the rudiments of knowledge
into the heads of largely unwilling subjects?*
*Where else can you find such large numbers
of people assembled in one building who collec-
tively care more about hair spray, car engines,
sex, the beach, clothes, sex, shoes that inflate
themselves, people who inflate themselves, sex,
zits, backstabbing, cheating, sex, and who is
going out with/cheating on/doing it with/used to
do it with/wants to do it with/claims to be doing
it with/and any other combination you can imagine, than they care about getting an education
that will prepare them for a productive future?*
*Go forth. (Gesture broadly.) Go forth and get
drunk, drive like maniacs, avoid responsibility,
hurt people's feelings, run over their mailboxes,
join fraternities, lust after the wrong people, and
otherwise refuse to live up to your potential.*
For those few of you who have set higher goals

for yourself in life, good luck in avoiding all the rest.

For those of you who just want to get out of here and head for the party, you'll be glad to know that this speech is over.

Thank you. (Bow humbly at standing ovation.)

Right, Starling. That speech might get you many things, but I doubted that a standing ovation was one of them.

Maybe it *would* be better if Jyl gave the speech.

Come to think of it, Starling's speech had potential. Maybe if I could just get him to focus a little more on the positive.

Actually, maybe I should just encourage him to give it. It certainly would make graduation memorable.

My mind was still occupied with Starling's speech when I stopped at my locker to drop off my physics book. I spun the combination lock, then opened the door. Hanging from a red ribbon was a large red heart, cut out of construction paper. I took it off the coat hook so that I could read what it said.

BETHANY,
HEARTS AND ROSES ARE NOT ENOUGH. I WANT TO INTRODUCE MY-SELF FACE-TO-FACE. I ONLY DARE

HOPE THAT YOU WILL SPARE ME THE TIME.

WOULD YOU BE SO KIND AS TO MEET ME NEXT WEDNESDAY NIGHT AT 8:00 P.M. ON THE FRONT STEPS OF MEMORIAL HALL ON THE UNIVERSITY OF DELAWARE CAMPUS?

MY COURAGE ONLY EXTENDS SO FAR AS YOU. PLEASE DO NOT INCLUDE ANYONE ELSE IN YOUR PLANS, OR I WILL NOT BELIEVE THAT YOU TRULY WANT TO MEET ME.

TRUST THAT I ONLY WANT THE BEST FOR YOU. TRUST THAT I WOULD NEVER DO ANYTHING TO HURT YOU, FOR THAT WOULD BE HURTING MYSELF AS WELL.

I searched both sides for a name, but there was none. What a weird note. At least it gave me the chance to end the mystery, though.

I couldn't wait to see what Starling thought.

Wait. If I told Starling, he'd insist on going with me. I know him. There's no way he'd stay away. If I didn't let him go with me, he'd be hiding in the bushes or riding by on a bicycle wearing a fake nose and a wig.

Maybe I shouldn't say a word to Starling.

Maybe I should just meet this person by myself and get some answers.

**TODAY IS THE DAY.
TODAY IT BEGINS.**

Chapter 13

The note threw me. I wasn't really sure what to do.

Tell my father? No way. It's not that I wouldn't trust him to understand, but he would overreact. If I told my father, he'd have the infantry surrounding the entire campus. Those military instincts die hard. Besides, he has so much on his mind with work these days that I hate to give him anything else to worry about. He might have to leave town again on short notice, and he wouldn't go if he thought that I needed help of any kind. Then he'd be even more pressured at work. No way could I tell my father.

Mr. Baldwin? There's another definite no. He's making a good recovery from the heart attack, and I don't want him to worry about a thing. Besides, he actually takes the puppy for walks now, and he only threatens to send it back to the SPCA about every other day. That's down from every day, so I'm optimistic.

The big question is Starling. I want to tell him. I think I'll explode if I don't at least mention it. I'm used to talking to him about anything, and this is definitely something. Lately he's been looking at me with this really curious expression, and I almost think that he can read my mind. He's even asked me if there's something bothering me, and I've had to fight real hard not to tell him.

I've looked at both sides over and over again. If I tell Starling, at least I'll have the presence of mind to know that he's around if I need him. It's not that Starling is some musclebound security guard or anything, but what he lacks in physical strength he makes up for in creativity. Plus I'll feel better when I'm not keeping secrets from him.

On the other hand, if I *do* tell Starling that I'd like to find out who my admirer is, I'm pretty sure he'll follow me and do something to give himself away. I don't think he'll agree to stay far enough away to guarantee that the person I'm meeting will believe that I'm alone. Besides, I'll have to live through all his plots to set up a surveillance system with remote microphones, cameras, and disguises. Starling would never settle for something as simple as staying within distant earshot.

There was one other possibility, but I wasn't giving it too much consideration. That was simply not to show up. I have to admit that I couldn't imagine doing that. Somebody had gone to a lot of trouble to make contact with me, and my curiosity was definitely captured. Most guys would just walk up and start a conversation or call the girl up or something normal like that. This guy was definitely being weird about this, and I wanted to know why. Besides, I needed to make some things clear to him.

I guess that meant Starling again. We haven't exactly proclaimed our undying love for each other, but we do really care about each other. In fact, we actually had sort of said we loved each other the night that Mr. Baldwin had his heart attack, but those circumstances were too stressful to really count.

What if this guy asked me out? I'd be flattered, but did I really want to go out with anybody but Starling? Part of me said yes, since Starling was the first guy I'd dated and maybe I should have some different experiences. What I couldn't face, though, was telling Starling that I wanted to go out with someone else. Wouldn't that mean that he was

then free to go out with someone else, too —
like Jyl, for instance?

Besides, this guy must be strange to go
through this whole red hearts and roses rou-
tine. Maybe he was about forty-seven years
old. Maybe he was hideously disfigured.
Maybe he was a psychopath who was going
to kidnap and rape and kill me.

Get a grip, Bethany. Your father didn't raise
you to be a fool. Memorial Hall is in the center
of the University of Delaware campus. The
University library is practically next to it, so
there're always people around. Besides, at this
time of year, it wouldn't even be dark yet.

I needed to meet him alone. I needed to
end all this suspense.

But what if he's crazy? What if he grabs me?

It's like being on a mental roller coaster. I'm
so sick of worrying about it that it's a major
relief that tonight's finally the night.

Plus I finally figured out a compromise.

Starling was a little surprised when I insisted
on going to the University library after we left
Mr. Baldwin's. I convinced him that the schol-
arly atmosphere was exactly what he needed
to work on revising his speech, *and* that I
really needed to study since exams were soon.

He suggested going to his house. He suggested going to my house. He suggested going

to a movie. I held out for the library.

Then came the tricky part. We were sitting in one of the second-floor conference rooms where we'd been working for the last hour. I must have looked at my watch a hundred times before it read a few minutes before eight.

"Starling, I need some fresh air before I start on this next chapter of physics," I said casually.

"I'll come with you."

"No," I protested quickly. "You're on a roll. You've been writing steadily, and I don't want to interrupt. I'll be back in a few minutes."

There must have been something weird in my voice because Starling looked at me carefully and shut his notebook. "It's no problem. I'm at a good breaking point. Some fresh air will do me good, too."

Great. Now what? I hadn't left enough time to deal with this.

"Starling, stop smothering me," I snapped. "Can't I even get a breath of fresh air without you hovering over me?" I hated saying those words, but I couldn't think of any other way. Then I thought again about what I was doing. "I'm just going to walk over to the steps of Memorial," I said. "I'll be back in five minutes." I didn't give him a chance to answer before I left the conference room and headed toward the stairs.

As soon as I turned a corner, I looked at my watch. Two minutes before eight. I took off at a sprint. The security guard at the desk frowned at me as I went past, but I showed him my empty hands and I didn't have a backpack or pocketbook with me to search. I was out the door and across the grass between the library and Memorial Hall before I gave myself any more time to think.

I rushed around the corner and came into view of the front steps of Memorial Hall. It is a two-story, colonial-looking red brick building with ivy growing on it, and the front steps are wide and white with black wrought-iron railings on either side.

Those steps were also empty.

I looked at my watch. It was exactly eight. I sat down on the third step and got my breath back. Five minutes. That's all he had to show up. Then I'd go back and face Starling.

Those were five agonizingly slow minutes. Several people walked nearby, but none of them approached the steps. A few squirrels raced up and down the elm tree near the steps, and a group of laughing guys crossed a sidewalk about fifty yards away, but that was it.

What was I going to say to Starling?

Before I left, I decided to walk to the top of the steps and take one last look. I trudged up slowly, filled with both disappointment and anger. This had been my night to get answers, and all I had now were more problems.

Right when I reached the top step, something caught my eye in the fading light.

There, pasted on the cement were red hearts. This time there were seventeen of them.

He had been here. But where was he now?

I straightened up and looked around.

The only person in the vicinity was Starling, standing at the bottom of the steps, looking up at me.

Chapter 14

"What's going on?" Starling asked quietly as he climbed the steps to me.

"You don't want to know," I said, sitting down and holding my head in my hands.

Then he must have seen the hearts. "You were going to meet him, weren't you?"

"Yes," I said.

"You got another note?" Starling was being deadly calm about this.

"Yes," I said.

"And you were just going to meet him here by yourself and take your chances?"

"Yes."

"Great plan, Bethany."

"Well, what was I supposed to do?" I asked, straightening up and looking out across the stretch of campus.

"You could have told me," Starling said.

"Right, so you could scare him away," I said

shortly, not meaning to be sharp with Starling, but so frustrated that I couldn't help it.

"Looks like you did a real good job by yourself," Starling said.

"Thanks," I said sarcastically.

"Bethany, you don't know this person. He could have meant you harm."

"I can take care of myself," I said forcefully.

"Oh, yes, the famous Bethany Anderson independence," Starling said.

"What's wrong with that?" I snapped.

"Nothing, unless you value your life," Starling said.

"You're being ridiculous. He's just some guy with a crush on me. You're building him up to be a mass murderer or something. I certainly am capable of meeting a guy, talking to him, and living to tell about it."

"And what were you going to say to him, Bethany?" This wasn't like Starling to be so serious, so quiet.

"I don't know. It depended on what he said to me."

"So if he said the right thing, you were going to say yes?"

"Starling, be reasonable. I wasn't going to go off with him or get in a car with him or agree to run away to Maryland and marry him.

I just wanted to meet him and clear up all the suspense."

"Are you sure that's all?"

"No, Starling, I wanted to make love here on the steps of Memorial Hall. There. Are you satisfied?"

"No," Starling said, still quietly. "No, I'm not satisfied at all. I can't believe you lied to me."

"I did not lie to you," I protested, knowing the argument was weak. Still, I'd prepared for this part since I knew I'd have to face it sooner or later. After all, I'd planned to tell Starling about the meeting after it was all over.

"Don't play word games with me," Starling said.

"I just withheld some information," I said. "I planned to tell you everything after I knew who this guy was."

"You should be a politician," Starling said.

"Low blow," I said, but he had a point. Usually I was brutally honest with him, and this skirting the truth was something new.

"I guess you simply don't trust me as much as I thought you did," Starling said. "And I guess you're more interested in meeting someone else than I counted on."

I could stand Starling yelling at me or cutting

me down or just about anything other than this quiet, hurt voice.

"Starling, I made a mistake. I'm sorry." I expected some reaction to that since I almost never apologize, but Starling didn't say a word. He simply started walking down the steps.

I went after him. After all, he had driven me here. Besides, I figured that once he got over this stage, we'd be able to talk it out.

Wrong.

We went back to the conference room and gathered our books in silence. We left the library and drove to my house in silence. It was horrible. The worst part was that I knew that Starling had a point. I hadn't been very honest with him, and I hadn't trusted him.

What made it even more terrible was the fact that I hadn't even learned the identity of my secret admirer.

Suddenly I hated red hearts and roses.

I got out of Starling's car and he promptly drove away. He always walks me in, but I guess he figured that I could take care of myself.

My father was reading in the living room, and I made polite conversation with him until I could escape to my room.

Great.

My secret admirer didn't admire me enough to show up.

Starling thought I was a jerk.

I thought I was a jerk.

I figured that the way life was going, right about now the puppy was peeing on Mr. Baldwin's sofa again, and even *he* thought I was a jerk for getting him a dog.

I tried to go back to studying physics, but I absolutely couldn't concentrate. Great. Now I'd fail my physics exam, and Mr. Clements would think I was a jerk.

Maybe I should just rent a billboard and display a huge message in red letters that said "Bethany Anderson is a jerk," and everybody could stand in front of it and cheer.

Get a grip, Bethany.

Okay.

I need to know who this red hearts and roses person is. I need to tell him that he is complicating my life and that the game is over.

I need to make things right with Starling.

I need a plan.

By sometime around two A.M. when I finally fell asleep, I was still searching for that plan.

At three A.M. the phone rang. I dashed down the hallway, picking up on the third ring. I was sure that it was Starling, feeling bad about our disagreement.

Silence greeted my repeated hellos.

At that moment I lost what little patience remained. "Are you the one who sent me flowers? Are you the one with the red hearts? Talk to me, damn it."

The phone clicked and the dial tone sounded in my ear. I slammed down the receiver.

And looked up to see my father standing in the doorway of his bedroom, staring at me.

Chapter 15

"Who were you talking to?" my father asked.

"Beats me," I said, my shoulders slumping.

"What was that about hearts and roses?"

I wasn't thinking very clearly. "Can we talk about this in the morning?" It was worth a try.

"Hearts and roses? Weren't the flowers from Starling?"

"No," I said. "And somebody has been pasting red hearts on my locker and sending me notes saying how wonderful I am." Everything I told my father was true, but as with Starling, it wasn't quite all.

"So somebody has a crush on you?" my father asked, visibly relaxing.

"Probably some silly underclassman," I said.

"And he called you at this ungodly hour of the night?" my father asked. He was definitely annoyed.

"I don't know." I was tired and startled, and that was the first thing that popped into my head.

"Could have just been a wrong number," my father reasoned.

"A wrong number who is now terribly confused," I said. "See you in the morning."

This time my father let me escape.

I went back to bed and lay there a second before I realized it was time to get up. Thursday. Great. Why couldn't it be Saturday so I didn't have to go to school? Why couldn't it be Saturday so I'd have the whole day to brood about how thoroughly I'd messed things up?

Why couldn't it be Saturday so I didn't have to face Starling?

Actually, I got part of what I wanted. Starling wasn't in school. Jyl asked me about him in physics, voice *full* of concern. I told her that as near as I knew he had a mild case of the bubonic plague, but he'd probably be back in school tomorrow. She looked confused, but she didn't ask me any more questions about Starling.

During lunch I lurked around the corner from my locker, watching for anyone suspicious. I felt like a fool, but I was desperate for information. Nothing.

After school I went to see Mr. Baldwin. I

put on what I thought was a cheerful face, determined not to let on that anything was wrong.

"Where's Mr. Whitman?" were the first words out of Mr. Baldwin's mouth.

Great start. "He's not here."

"I can see that, Miss Anderson. I may be recovering from a heart attack, but I'm not blind and stupid."

"He wasn't in school today," I amended.

"And you don't know why?"

"No," I admitted.

"What are you two disagreeing about?" Mr. Baldwin asked with a sigh.

I looked at him in amazement. It's not like him to get involved in emotional matters.

"It's a long, stupid story," I said. "We'll work it out." I really didn't want to go into it with Mr. Baldwin. He'd think I was a blathering adolescent idiot, which was just about how I felt. I needed to change the subject. "How's Anna?" I asked innocently.

"How would I know?" Mr. Baldwin answered.

"You don't go for walks with her?" I asked.

"Do I look like a glutton for punishment?" Mr. Baldwin responded. "First I have had this beast imposed upon me, and now I have an interfering, domineering woman telling me how to breathe. Ah, for the days when all I had to cope with were 150 hormone-ridden adolescents to whom I was supposed to teach the intricacies of history."

The "beast" was romping across the living room floor, chasing the ball that I was tossing for him. Of course he didn't bring the ball back, but rather took it into other rooms, left it there, and then came back and looked at me as if I had stolen it. At least my expeditions to find the ball gave me time to think of answers for Mr. Baldwin.

"Does the puppy need to go for a walk, then?" I asked.

"We've walked. In fact, we walked several times. It saves the rugs and furniture," Mr. Baldwin said pointedly.

"But without Anna — uh, excuse me," I said. I got up to search for the ball under the china cabinet in the dining room.

"How do you manage to avoid her?" I asked after I'd given the puppy the ball.

"There are ways," Mr. Baldwin said smugly. "Luckily I don't particularly mind being an early riser."

"How early?" I asked suspiciously.

"By walking at five-thirty A.M., I have found myself able to avoid unwanted companions,"

Mr. Baldwin said, sounding satisfied with himself.

"Five-thirty in the morning?" I asked in amazement. "You voluntarily get up that early to avoid Anna?"

"And to walk the beast. Yes. Air quality is better at that hour, also. Undisturbed by the rattle and hubbub of humanity. Much of humanity's purest thinking has been done in the early hours."

Great. Maybe that's what I needed to do. Ponder my problems at dawn.

"And then you walk later, too?" I asked, pleased that even if his attitude was still surly, at least he was getting more exercise.

"Purely for biological necessity," Mr. Baldwin said, watching as "the beast" charged across the floor, skidded, and ended up sliding into the wall. I think I almost saw a smile. Almost.

"And you don't run into Anna?"

"Out the back, around by that small area that the city fathers grace with the misnomer of park, and back home without crossing her path," he said.

"You and the beast," I said with a smile. The puppy had finally exhausted itself and had curled up in my lap.

"We need to talk about that," Mr. Baldwin said, clearing his throat.

Oh, no. On top of everything else, Mr. Baldwin was going to make me take the puppy back to the SPCA. I couldn't stand it. I absolutely, positively couldn't stand it.

"No, Mr. Baldwin. Please don't tell me that," I said.

"Tell you that the beast needs a proper name?"

I looked at him, relief flooding me. This was it. He had given in. The puppy was safe. At least one small part of my life was working out.

"You're definitely going to keep him?" I said.

"I will have you know that this is against my better judgment, and I am going to hold you personally liable for any damage that this creature does," Mr. Baldwin announced.

"Fine," I said. If he asked me for five hundred dollars for a new sofa, I'd find a way.

"And I want you to know how transparent and insulting this whole maneuver has been. Allergies and memories, my eye."

"I just wanted you to have some company, and I wanted this puppy to have a good home," I said, looking at the floor.

"If I had wanted company, I would have provided it myself," Mr. Baldwin said, but his eyes softened just a tiny bit as he looked at the puppy.

"Sorry."

"Still, the beast has added a certain amount of annoyance to my daily existence which, I suppose, keeps the blood flowing," Mr. Baldwin said.

I smiled. That was as close to a declaration of love as he'd ever give.

"Besides, I would never consider giving that woman the satisfaction of believing I couldn't control a mop of fur and bones," Mr. Baldwin huffed.

Thank you, Anna, I thought silently.

"And now he needs a name," I said.

"It seems only proper," Mr. Baldwin replied.

"What about Beast?" I suggested. I looked down at the little dog, his wiry coat sticking up in random tufts.

"I don't want to give him that much credit," Mr. Baldwin said. "And I refuse to have any of those sickening animal names that are an embarrassment to say in public."

"Fluffy?" I suggested. "Poopsy? Doodles?"

"If you mention Snookums, I shall be forced to ask you to leave," Mr. Baldwin said.

"Okay, how about some historical names?" I said. I transferred the puppy from my lap to

Mr. Baldwin's. The puppy looked up at him quizzically.

"Napoleon?" Mr. Baldwin asked the puppy. The puppy didn't respond. "Churchill? Tutankhamen? Caesar?" The puppy sighed.

Suddenly I was overcome by a sense of loss. Starling should be here. He'd be great at this. I tried to focus my mind on names again. "Rex? Rover? Have there been any famous dogs in history?" I asked.

"Possibly the wolf that supposedly suckled Romulus and Remus in the days of ancient civilization," Mr. Baldwin answered, "but I don't recall its name."

"Okay, let's think of names of students you didn't like," I suggested.

"Why would I want to recall those multitudes?" Mr. Baldwin asked.

"People you admire, then." I was getting desperate.

"Michelangelo." Mr. Baldwin was on a roll. "Da Vinci. Mozart, Machiavelli. FDR."

"That's it!" I shouted.

"You propose I should name this animal FDR?" Mr. Baldwin responded. The puppy was staring at him, cocking his head.

"No. Mozart," I said happily.

"Mozart?" Mr. Baldwin said. He looked at the puppy. "Here, Mozart," he tried. "That sounds ridiculous," he said. "I might as well name him Mussolini."

"How about his first name?" I wasn't giving up.

"This animal has to have a first name and a last name?" Mr. Baldwin asked, thoroughly confused.

"No, Mr. Baldwin — Mozart's first name," I explained.

"Wolfgang Amadeus?" Mr. Baldwin said.

"Just Wolfgang would do," I said. "Isn't that a great name?"

"Wolfgang," Mr. Baldwin tried, looking at the puppy. Then he repeated it several times with greater authority.

I wish I could report that the puppy immediately came to attention and barked or something. Actually, all he did was lie down and go to sleep.

Still, that was one problem solved. It was the perfect name.

I said good-bye to Mr. Baldwin and Wolfgang after making sure they were both set for dinner. As I headed out to my car, I realized that it felt funny to be leaving alone.

What I saw next wasn't funny at all.

As I got into my car and got ready to drive away, something caught my eye.

There on the windshield were three red hearts.

WHY DID SHE DO THAT?

WHY DID SHE ARRIVE AT THE LIBRARY
   WITH ANOTHER, WHEN I TOLD HER
   TO COME ALONE?

DID SHE ACTUALLY THINK I WOULDN'T
   KNOW?

WHY DOESN'T SHE SEE THE TRUTH?
   WHY DOESN'T SHE SEE THAT HE IS
   MERELY A FRAUD, BUT I AM THE ONE
   WHO NEEDS HER, LOVES HER?

I SHALL HAVE TO MAKE HER SEE THE
   TRUTH.

Chapter 16

At first I was alarmed by the hearts on my windshield; then I was furious.

Who was this person to follow me? What made him think he had the right to intrude on my life? What made him think that spying on me was the way to get my attention?

I'd find him. I didn't know how, but I'd find him, and when I did, he'd get a piece of my mind that he wouldn't soon forget.

I drove home in a fit of anger, barely remembering to stop for red lights. My father's car wasn't in the driveway, but it was still early. My anger gave me plenty of energy, and I decided I'd fix a dinner for my father that required plenty of shredding and mashing and pounding.

As I got out of the car, I scraped the hearts off the windshield. If that creep was spying on me, he'd see what I thought of his feeble attempts at decoration. I stomped up the driveway, ducking around the bushes to the front door to get the mail. That's when my mood changed rather abruptly.

There was an envelope in the mailbox along with the weekly flyer from Acme and a large manila envelope addressed to my father. The regular envelope just said BETHANY in large square letters.

I knew that printing.

I ripped it open. I remember thinking there had to be a clue, something that would lead me to him.

Inside were two pictures. They were color snapshots, and they featured two of my favorite people.

One was Starling.

One was Jyl.

They were sitting at a table in the University of Delaware library. Jyl had her chair pulled right up next to Starling's, and they were looking down at the book they were sharing.

How cozy. In one of the pictures, Jyl had her hand on the back of Starling's neck.

He sure hadn't wasted any time, had he?

Wait. I was assuming that these pictures were taken last night or something. Maybe they'd been taken a while ago. I studied both shots carefully. No, Starling was wearing the shirt his mother had bought him last weekend. Definitely recent. After all, there were plenty of one-hour film developing places around.

I had been so busy studying the pictures that I ignored the note that was with them, but eventually I got to that, too.

BETHANY,
WHY DIDN'T YOU GO TO THE LIBRARY ALONE? WHY DID YOU GO WITH HIM, RATHER THAN COME TO MEET ME BY YOURSELF? HE DOESN'T CARE ABOUT YOU, NOT THE WAY I DO.
THAT WAS MEANT TO BE OUR TIME.
I TRUSTED YOU, BUT YOU BETRAYED THAT TRUST.
WHY?
WHAT MUST I DO TO PROVE TO YOU THAT I AM WORTHY OF YOUR CONSIDERATION?
WHAT PROOF DO YOU NEED?

My mind was reeling! I wanted to tell him to try stopping this campaign to drive me stark, raving mad. Try showing up at my doorstep like a normal human being and just talking to me. Try not sending me pictures that I really don't want to see.

Still, I couldn't help staring at the photos.

Starling and Jyl. Great. That was a sight I wanted to pin on my wall to enjoy at my leisure.

I went back to the kitchen door, checked it for red hearts, and unlocked it. I opened the fridge and started checking out foods to mutilate for dinner.

I made chicken cordon bleu because I got to pound the chicken breasts. I made a tossed salad because I got to rip the lettuce and chop the tomatoes and peppers. I made mashed potatoes, without the electric mixer.

I didn't feel like explaining when my father asked me to what we owed this deluxe dinner. I just didn't want to talk about it.

"When is your graduation?" He was trying to break the ice.

The funny thing was that I actually had to stop and think. "Ten days from today," I muttered.

I'd looked forward to graduation for practically my whole life, and now I could barely remember when it was.

"I'll be there," my father said proudly. "You know I'd never miss your big day."

"I'd understand." I looked down at my plate while saying those dutiful daughter words, but I didn't really mean them. I couldn't imagine not having anyone in the audience who cared about me.

"I'll be there," my father repeated. "I'll talk to the boss tomorrow and see what kind of schedule we can work out — in fact, I'll do some of the preliminary work on the report this evening." He stood up and smiled. "Great dinner."

With that he was gone. I cleared the table and loaded the dishwasher. My brain felt like it was going to explode. If I had told my father *everything,* he wouldn't have left for California. I hadn't wanted that. And what if nothing happened? Then I'd feel like a fool for interfering with his work. Right now, some geek was probably laughing hysterically about how he'd strung me along. Maybe this was just a late April Fools' joke or part of a fraternity initiation rite.

The weirdest thing was that Starling wasn't around anymore.

This time I'd just have myself.

And that would have to be enough.

Chapter 17

The next day at school I didn't see Starling until physics. I had considered all kinds of possibilities, and I had decided to simply apologize to him.

Something happened to that plan when I finally saw Starling. Maybe it had something to do with the fact that Jyl seemed to be attached to him with Velcro.

Luckily, for both of them, the bell rang for class and she went to her own seat. I sat down next to Starling. Mr. Clements immediately began class, reviewing for the exam. I reached into my backpack and pulled out the pictures of Starling and Jyl and threw them down in front of Starling. Then I pulled out my notebook and acted like I was interested in Mr. Clements' calculations.

I saw Starling pick up the pictures and carefully examine them. "Where did you get these?" he whispered.

"Where do you think?" I hissed.

"Bethany, I'm serious."

"So am I. They were in my mailbox with a note."

Starling just looked at me. I reached into my backpack and pulled out the note. Starling threw it down after he read it.

"That does it," he said, his voice tense.

What was he mad about now? Was I being held responsible for this, too?

"What?" I demanded. "Don't you think it's a good picture of Jyl?"

"Excuse me, Bethany and Starling. Am I interrupting something by conducting class up here?"

Mr. Clements. We had completely forgotten about him.

"Excuse *us*, Mr. Clements, but there's been an emergency. We need to leave." Starling stood up, grabbed his books, and reached for my hand.

"But we're reviewing for the exam." Mr. Clements looked like we'd hurt his feelings. He *really* loves his physics.

"We'll bring you a note," Starling mumbled.

A note? From whom? From this nut case who was following me? What did Starling mean, we'd bring a note? Besides, why did we have to leave right *now*?

"Come on," Starling said firmly. I didn't think this was a very good idea, but I didn't feel like discussing it in front of the entire class.

"You will bring me an official pass," Mr. Clements ordered as we ran from the room.

"Absolutely," Starling said over his shoulder. With that, we were standing in the hallway.

"Would you mind telling me what is going on?" I asked. Starling was walking briskly down the hallway, and I had to hustle to keep up with him.

"I've had it with this," Starling said sharply.

"Well, I'm not exactly thrilled myself, but why did we have to walk out of class?" I asked.

"Because we're going to the police, that's why."

"Starling, we are *not* going to the police."

"Oh, yes, we are."

"On what grounds? Are you going to claim that your rights were violated because someone took a picture of you and your precious Jyl?"

"Let's get something straight right now, Bethany," Starling said, his voice icy. "This has *nothing* to do with Jyl."

"Looks to me like it does — looks like she

moved right in." I tried to bite my tongue, but the words had already slipped out.

"I don't owe you an explanation, but I'll give you one," Starling said. By this time we were in the parking lot heading for his car. "I went to the library to work on my speech. Jyl happened to be there, too."

"Just happened to be there?" I said sarcastically. "What a coincidence."

Starling ignored me. "I helped her with a physics problem, and then I asked her if she would mind leaving me to my work. She left."

"Sure," I said.

"It's the truth, whether you believe it or not."

I studied Starling's face carefully. There was absolutely no sign of teasing or deceit. I believed him. "Then what are these pictures?"

"Obviously this person was watching me, and he took them during those few minutes."

"How?" I asked.

"I wasn't in a conference room," Starling explained. "They were all filled, so I was sitting out at a table. There are rows and rows of books all around there, so I probably wouldn't have seen somebody there with a camera."

"This gives me the creeps." I could feel the goose bumps beginning to perk up on my arms.

"And that's why we're going to the police." He unlocked the passenger door of Dinosaur for me, got in, and started the car.

"Starling, I want this to stop, too, but I don't see how the police will take us seriously."

"We are law-abiding citizens, and we're being harassed."

"But what has he done that makes it a police concern?" I was trying to be rational. "What laws has he broken?"

"That's what I want to find out."

"So we're just going to cruise into the police station and ask?" This whole thing was getting more than a little out of control.

"Yes," Starling said flatly.

"What if they laugh at us?"

"Then they laugh."

I couldn't think of much of a response to that, so I shut up. I really wasn't looking forward to this, but at least Starling was talking to me again. If that meant going to the police station, so be it.

The Newark police station is a cement bunkerlike building on Main Street with a blue sign over its door. Its most dramatic features were the cop cars parked beside it. I started to make one more attempt at getting Starling to change his mind, but I took one look at his face and gave up. Usually Starling looks like he might smile or make a wisecrack at any second; this time he looked somber.

Okay. Maybe this would be a good idea. Maybe the police could track down this person and end this right now.

Sure.

Starling and I walked in the front door. I have to admit that it made me a little bit nervous. I mean, I knew I wasn't a criminal or anything, but I've seen too many of those movies where innocent people are thrown into jail. I've always hated the sound of that barred cell door clanging shut. Maybe I would walk into the police station, and there, in the wanted posters, would be a face that looked just like mine.

Maybe I have an overactive imagination.

"May I help you?" asked the bored-looking policeman behind the counter. He had a telephone plastered to one ear.

"We have a problem," Starling said politely.

"Planned Parenthood is one block over," the policeman answered with a smirk.

I looked at the cop in disbelief. Maybe we'd just been shot or robbed or something, and this guy was making snide comments about our sex lives?

Even Starling didn't see any humor in this. "That is *definitely* not our problem."

"Joke," the policeman said. "Just a joke."

If we wanted comedy, we would have gone to a movie or something. I wasn't too thrilled with our introduction to the justice system.

"Let's just go." I grabbed Starling's hand and pulled him in the direction of the door.

With that, the policeman put down the phone. "What's the problem?"

I wasn't in the mood to discuss this with him. Starling would have to do it.

"Someone is following us." Starling dropped my hand and turned around.

"Is that right?" the policeman smirked. "How do you know this?"

"He leaves notes and other indications," Starling fired back.

"How do you know it's a *he*?" asked the policeman. "Have you seen this person?"

"No, but he's definitely interested in Bethany," Starling answered.

The policeman looked like he was going to say something smart, but the phone rang again and he answered it.

"This isn't going too well," I whispered.

The policeman hung up the phone. "So. Somebody has the hots for your girlfriend."

"Somebody follows her, writes notes asking her to meet him, and even follows me and takes pictures," Starling said. I could hear the anger in his voice, but I guess the policeman either didn't notice or didn't care.

"Ain't young love grand?" he smirked again. "Now me, I'm divorced three times, so nothing surprises me these days."

Great. We have to run into somebody who figures love rots no matter what.

"Are we entitled to file a complaint?" Starling asked.

"Has this person threatened you, approached you, harmed you or your property?"

"Not exactly," I answered.

"Then you have no grounds for a complaint," the officer replied bluntly.

"What does he have to do?" Starling was really getting mad.

"Come after you in a way that endangers you," the policeman answered, sounding bored.

"So as long as he invades my privacy and drives me nuts, there's nothing you can do?" I asked.

"That's about it," he said. The phone rang again, and he turned away from us.

I looked at Starling and shook my head. We walked out of the police station and got into the car.

"That was really helpful." I wanted to say I

told you so, but I didn't think that would be a very good move.

"We'll just have to come up with a plan," Starling said.

Oh, no. Not a Starling-Horace-Whitman-the-Fifth plan. These always have a way of getting out of hand.

"Starling, maybe he'll just give up. Maybe if he sees us together and realizes that the pictures didn't make me hate you or something, he'll just pick somebody else."

"Do you really believe that?" Starling asked.

"Sure."

Starling looked at me as if I'd sprouted a second head.

"Okay, maybe not," I admitted.

"We have to find a way to make him do something." Starling was on a roll.

"Great plan," I said. "Let's get him to hurt one of us so that the police will have to do something."

"That's not what I mean. We have to get him close enough to find out who he is."

"How are we supposed to do that?" I was getting frustrated. "We can't exactly call him up and invite him over for pizza and a friendly game of Trivial Pursuit."

"When was the last time he was close to

you?" Starling demanded. "We need to chart his activities."

"Starling, I don't even know who he is. How am I supposed to know where he is and what he's doing?"

"We have to be logical about this."

"Could we be logical somewhere else?" I asked, since we were still sitting in the police station parking lot. "If our friendly neighborhood policeman sees us, he'll probably arrest us for loitering."

Starling started the car and we pulled out of the parking lot. He drove down to the end of Main Street and found a parking place. I knew where he was going. There are big old trees on the section of campus that comes up to town, and it's one of our favorite places to sit. I was right. Starling got out of the car.

"Bring some paper," he called back to me.

I grabbed my backpack and followed him.

Starling threw himself down on the ground and looked up at the sky. "Now," he said, "we need to list the contacts he's made, where they've taken place, and what time of day. Make a chart with columns."

Usually I wouldn't have let him order me around like that, but I humored him this time. I opened a notebook to a clean sheet of paper and made three columns with headings that said contact, location, and time.

"Okay, Beach, when did you first become aware of him?"

"When those red hearts appeared on my locker," I said. "Remember? I thought you had done it."

Starling looked at me. "But *I* didn't. Write it down."

Feeling stupid, I wrote in the first column, "Red hearts on locker."

"Where?" Starling asked, staring up at the sky.

"On my locker," I sighed.

"Put school," Starling said, not paying attention to my sarcasm. "Time?"

"How am I supposed to know?"

"When had you last been to your locker?"

"When I left school the day before, I guess."

"And when did you find the hearts?"

"After homeroom," I said. "You were there."

"Put two-twenty P.M. to eight A.M.," Starling said smugly. Great Detective Starling.

We went through it all that way. It was surprisingly difficult to get the sequence exactly right, and to remember if we saw something after homeroom or after physics or after lunch or whatever. Finally we had a list: hearts on locker; hearts on kitchen door; rose in locker with note; dozen roses and note with hearts at home; possibly an additional heart on kitchen door; heart note asking for meeting; hearts on the steps of Memorial Hall; hearts on the windshield when I left Mr. Baldwin's; and the note and pictures in the mailbox. We did our best to figure out the time frames, and I also told Starling about the weird phone calls.

"We don't know for sure that the calls are from him," Starling deduced.

"On the list or not?" I was quite proud of the chart now that it was done.

"Special note at the bottom," Detective Starling answered.

He sat up and studied the notebook page. "Now we have to find a pattern," he said, looking over the chart carefully.

The only pattern I could see was those damnable hearts.

Starling studied the chart with complete concentration for minute after silent minute. Finally he handed it back to me.

"Okay." He smiled. "I've got a plan."

WITHOUT HER, THERE IS NO HOPE.
THERE IS NO WARMTH IN A COLD AND
   HOSTILE WORLD.
THERE IS NO REASON TO BELIEVE
   THAT THE STARS WILL SHINE AT
   NIGHT, OR THAT I WILL EXIST TO SEE
   THEM.
WITHOUT HER, I WILL NEVER AGAIN
   BELIEVE THAT LOVE CAN EXIST,
   THAT HEARTS CAN BE TRUE, OR
   THAT HAPPINESS IS ANYTHING MORE
   THAN A CHILDISH CHARADE.
WITHOUT BETHANY, I HAVE NO REA-
   SON OR MEANING.

SHE MUST SEE ME.
SHE MUST GIVE ME REASON TO HOPE.
SHE MUST GIVE ME REASON TO LIVE.

Chapter 18

"Starling, cut the suspense crap. What's the plan?"

"It's not very elaborate." Starling sounded disappointed.

"That's a relief," I said. "Your elaborate plans would probably involve a budget the size of the Defense Department's and a cast of thousands."

"This one involves just me."

"Oh, no, you don't," I said quickly, before he could go any further. "This is my problem, and I'm going to be involved in solving it."

"Bethany, can't you just step back a little bit and let me handle this?"

"No."

"Never mind," Starling said. "You're in this plan, anyway. I just meant that this doesn't involve anybody other than me helping you."

"Oh." I guess I had jumped on him rather quickly. "So what's the plan?"

"I figure this person knows the logical places to find you — school, home, Mr. Baldwin's."

I had to figure out that whole list of contacts for Starling to come up with that? I wasn't impressed.

"So all I need to do is watch you from a distance when you're at those places, and I'll be able to watch him watch you, and then we'll figure out who he is."

"That's it? You're going to spy on me? It isn't bad enough that I have one person spying on me, but now I'm going to have two?"

"Yes, but one of them will be a friendly spy." Starling reached over to pat my back.

"Great." I rolled my eyes. "Why don't I just get a movie camera, film my life, and play it on a big screen for everyone to watch?"

"Camera. Not a bad idea." Starling grinned.

"Stop. Forget I said that. Besides, how will this work? How will you know where to be so that you won't scare him away? Besides, Starling, he knows who *you* are. If he sees you, he'll figure out what you're doing."

"Not to worry," Starling exclaimed. "I have my ways!"

I knew it. Starling was not going to be happy

until he was wearing disguises and hiding in bushes.

"Starling, you're not exactly low profile. To begin with, you have the most obvious car in the world."

Starling looked toward the car. "Dinosaur? Come on, Bethany, you know there must be hundreds of olive-green Plymouth Furies in Newark."

"Then how come I haven't seen a single one except yours?" I asked. "Answer me that, Mr. Wise Guy."

"Your powers of observation are obviously lacking."

I punched him in the stomach, not hard enough to make him throw up but hard enough to get his attention. He grabbed my arms and wrestled me until he thought he had me pinned. I got free when he relaxed his grip and rolled away. I laughed gleefully, and Starling rolled up into a ball, looking like an overgrown anteater. It felt good to joke around again, to be comfortable with each other.

Starling smiled and took my hand. "Trust me. I'll figure out who this person is."

"And then what?"

"And then you can decide what to do about him."

That was exactly the right answer, and I

gave a startled Starling a big kiss. It took a while before we talked any more.

"I'm not complaining, but what was that for?" Starling finally asked.

"That was for acknowledging that this is my problem, and I should have some say in resolving it," I answered.

"I hope you know how difficult it is to restrain my masculine impulses," Starling said, eyes twinkling. "After all, my greatest desire is to find this punk and beat the crap out of him, leaving him at your feet a whimpering mass of pulverized flesh. Then you'll see me for the stud that I am, and fall into my arms in gratitude, asking what you can do to reward me."

The best I could do for Starling at that moment was to keep a straight face and say, "Right, Starling." I mean, Starling is fit and wiry, but he will never be a body double for Stallone or Schwarzenegger.

" . . . but in deference to you, I'll leave him alive and unbroken," Starling continued as if I hadn't spoken. Then his voice turned more serious. "I just want to know that he's not dangerous. I'm sure he's just some guy who's attracted to you for all the reasons that I am, but I want you to have the chance to do whatever it is that you want to do — talk to him, tell him to leave you alone, marry him, whatever."

"I don't plan to marry him, Starling."

"Well, that's a relief," Starling said, wiping his brow dramatically. "Look, there's one more part to my plan that might speed things up."

I was all in favor of doing anything I could to resolve this once and for all. "What's that?"

"It might encourage him to make contact again if he thought that we weren't seeing each other anymore."

I didn't especially like the idea, but it made sense. Suddenly I had a weird thought. "Starling, what if he's watching us right now?"

Starling and I pulled away from each other and looked around. All at once, every tree was cover for someone standing behind it, and every male walking down the sidewalk could possibly be him.

"We've already set the plan back by kissing," Starling muttered. "Why don't you slap me or something?"

Now there was a tempting offer, but something else was more tempting. "No, if we have to act mad at each other, this might be the last time I'll get to do this," I said.

I kissed Starling until his glasses fogged over. He cooperated fully.

"I sure am sorry I have to hate your guts," I said quietly.

We kissed some more as we planned when and where to fight.

Life sure is weird sometimes.

Still, on a hot Delaware day in early June, with the sun glowing on our faces and a light sheen of sweat on our backs, we laughed and joked and schemed.

After all, this was all some big game, anyway.

Wasn't it?

Chapter 19

We decided to go visit Mr. Baldwin while we could still go together. When we got there, he was puttering around in the kitchen, complaining about the lack of red meat in the house. I took this as a good sign. If he was hungry and feisty, he must be nearly recovered.

Starling and I left him to his disgusted tirade about yet another piece of boneless, skinless chicken, and took Wolfgang for a walk. Actually, we took him for a romp. We figured he had plenty of disciplined, lecture-filled walks. We wanted him to just be a puppy and play.

We ended up in the park near Mr. Baldwin's house. Wolfgang seemed familiar with it, probably from all the times he and Mr. Baldwin had gone there while hiding out from Anna. Starling unhooked the puppy's leash and took off at a run, Wolfgang leaping at his heels, jumping up at him and yipping madly. I laughed, hoping

Wolfgang had the good sense not to try any of this with Mr. Baldwin.

After a few minutes, a slightly winded Starling came sprinting back, a perfectly fresh Wolfgang at his heels. He picked up the puppy and covered its eyes.

"Go hide," Starling whispered.

"What?"

"Go and hide. Let's see if this dog has any tracking capabilities."

"Starling, he's just a little puppy. He's not a bloodhound or something." Wolfgang was squirming in Starling's arms.

"We'll never know until we try. He might be a long-lost relative of some heroic police dog, or one of those Saint Bernards that save people in the mountains."

"Starling, look at him. Do you see any Saint Bernard blood in him?" I figured I had a pretty good argument there. The puppy weighed maybe four pounds and was nothing but tufts of fur and big brown eyes.

"A very *small* breed of Saint Bernard," Starling said smugly. He wasn't going to give up. "Will you please just go hide?"

"Fine — get rid of me, why don't you? It'll be next week before Wolfgang finds me."

I felt like a fool, but I walked about twenty feet away and leaned against the far side of a huge oak tree. I could hear Starling talking to the puppy.

"Wolfgang, find Bethany." I peeked around the tree in time to see Wolfgang leap up and nip at Starling's butt. Good Wolfgang.

"No, Wolfgang, find Bethany." Starling gave him an encouraging shove. The only problem was that the puppy was headed in the opposite direction from where I stood, and he was chasing down a leaf caught in the breeze. I stifled a laugh. Starling went after the puppy, picked him up, and had a very serious talk with him that I couldn't fully hear.

"Now, Wolfgang, find Bethany." This time Wolfgang at least headed in my direction. Of course, he veered off seven or eight times before he actually found me, and I think it was more luck than tracking, but eventually he came dashing up to me, tail wagging.

I, of course, praised him lavishly. When Starling came to join us, I tried to look serious. "Maybe we should ask Mr. Baldwin to change his name to Sherlock."

"Try it again," Starling said.

This time I hid at the top of a sliding board, which I suppose was pretty tricky of me, and it only took Wolfgang about four false starts before he stood barking up at me.

By the fourth time, even I was convinced

that Wolfgang had just a little bit of tracking blood in him. Of course, it also could have been the fact that I found some peppermint Life Savers in my pocket and kept feeding them to him.

I never saw a dog before that liked peppermint.

All three of us were hot and panting by the time we got home. I figured that at least Mr. Baldwin should have a quiet evening with Wolfgang since I doubted he had the energy to cause any trouble.

We walked in the door to the sound of a woman's voice. It was unmistakably Anna's.

"Seth, you need just a touch of rosemary, not that boring parsley. Not that I mean to tell you how to cook."

"Then don't," Mr. Baldwin snapped back.

"Now I have been cooking chicken for years with rosemary, and everybody raves about it," Anna continued, as if Mr. Baldwin had not just cut her off. "So you may just appreciate the fact that I have my areas of knowledge, just as you have yours."

"And what do you consider to be my areas of knowledge, since you certainly seem to feel free to criticize my every move?"

"Well, it's certainly not raising a puppy," Anna replied with a hearty laugh.

With that, Wolfgang headed for the kitchen, Starling and I behind him, trying not to laugh.

Wolfgang went straight for his water bowl, which he lapped dry. Then he went and sat at Mr. Baldwin's feet, looking up at him seriously.

Mr. Baldwin looked down at the puppy. "Would you like more water?" he asked. The puppy whined softly. Mr. Baldwin got the dish, filled it, and put it down for Wolfgang, who drank more before going over to the far corner of the kitchen and throwing himself down on the cool tile floor.

"And what seems to be wrong with the way I'm raising this animal?" Mr. Baldwin asked. I'm sure he knew how lucky he'd been with Wolfgang; the puppy just as easily could have jumped up on Anna or tried to scale the kitchen counter.

"I think it's a testimony to the sweet nature of that poor little thing," Anna said firmly.

The "poor little thing" stretched out on his back, all four feet up in the air, looking like a very contented corpse.

"Seth, now what do you think you're doing with that broccoli?"

Starling and I waved good-bye to Mr. Baldwin and beat a hasty retreat. As we got to the door, we heard Anna telling Mr. Baldwin what sweet children we are. Mr. Baldwin's snort echoed all the way from the kitchen. Somehow we managed to keep from laughing until we got to the car.

Starling took me home. We searched carefully for hearts or notes, but everything was normal. I was almost disappointed. My father's car wasn't in the driveway, but it was earlier than I had thought. After all, Starling and I had made a rather early departure from school and — uh-oh . . .

"Starling, what about that note you promised Mr. Clements to explain why we left class? And what about the rest of our classes?"

"Don't worry. I'll forge one."

"Starling, we're days away from graduating. Don't get us in trouble now."

"What do you suggest?"

"Maybe I could get my dad to write one."

"Are you going to tell him the whole story?"

That made me stop to think. "No, not exactly that," I said. "Maybe I'll tell him I didn't feel good. That's pretty close to the truth."

Starling grinned. "And I'll say that I had sympathetic pain since we have a psychic bond between us."

"Maybe Mr. Clements will forget," I continued. "After all, exams start tomorrow."

"That's right," Starling said. "And because of the exam schedule, we won't have his class tomorrow. Besides, he's almost rid of us. Do you really think he wants to write us up and go through all the paperwork?"

I guessed there was a slim chance that Starling was right.

We got out of the car and walked into the house. It was a habit now to check for hearts on the door.

There was a note from my father on the kitchen table.

Bethany —
By leaving for California this afternoon, I can get home for graduation. Sorry for the short notice — new problems with the project. Don't you need a dress or something for graduation? I left money under the sugar bowl. I <u>will</u> be home to see you graduate.

Love,
Dad

My father knocks me out. Just when you think he's totally preoccupied with work, he remembers something like a dress for graduation, which is more than I had done, since I hadn't even thought about what you were supposed to wear under those silly gowns. I looked under the sugar bowl. He'd left fifty dollars. I supposed I'd have to go shopping. I hate shopping. Actually, I hate dresses, too.

Starling stayed for dinner, and then we studied for exams.

Really. We did study.

Most of the time.

Chapter 20

What is it they say about three strikes?

First of all, I had to take my first two exams. They weren't terrible, but they were long and tiring. Whatever I didn't know, I blamed on Starling.

Second of all, it was part of the plan to break up with Starling.

Third of all, I had to go shopping. For a dress.

I think I'll just go to bed. The only problem is that I have two more exams tomorrow, which I really should study for, and I can't even be distracted by Starling along the way. I hate this. I hate the red heart jerk who created these problems — or at least some of them. I would have had to take exams and buy a dress even if none of this had happened.

Still, breaking up with Starling was a pain. Starling wanted to do it at school during lunch in front of hundreds of people. He even wanted me to buy spaghetti for lunch and throw it at him. He said that if I ever doubted his concern for my well-being, I should remember that offer.

I refused. Even though I only have a few days of high school left, I want to leave without making a public spectacle of myself. Can't you just see it — the talk of the school for all the wrong reasons. The only temptation was that I had a sneaking suspicion that Starling would look kind of attractive with spaghetti dripping off his glasses, but still I wouldn't do it.

Besides, Jyl would probably be there, and I couldn't stand to watch her consoling Starling.

We compromised on doing it both in the school parking lot and in front of my house. As we walked out of school, I started quietly yelling at Starling.

"I'm sick of your attitude. What makes you think you can rule my life?"

"What makes you so stubborn, hard-headed, arrogant, and insensitive?" Starling yelled back. I was impressed. That had all flowed right out.

"What makes you think I need *you* or anybody else?" I said, stomping away from him.

"Come back here," Starling hollered after

me, running to catch up. "How are you going to get home?"

"I'll walk," I said, hoping he wouldn't take me up on that. Needless to say, anybody within earshot was glued to the action. I just hoped Mr. Red Hearts was lurking somewhere in the vicinity.

"We'll finish this discussion on the way home," Starling said firmly as he got to Dinosaur.

"Fine," I said, getting in and slamming the door. Starling started the engine and tried to screech out of the parking lot. Dinosaur definitely does not screech.

Once we were out of sight, I slumped back in the seat, exhausted.

"That was kind of fun, wasn't it?" Starling said.

"Fun? Did you get your kicks calling me hard-headed and arrogant? Did it feel good?"

"Bethany, calm down. Don't start a fight for real. Of course you're not hard-headed."

"So you're saying that I am arrogant?"

"Save it for in front of your house," Starling said with a laugh.

I took a few deep breaths and settled down. I guess I was just a little tense.

Round two came in my driveway.

I slammed out of the car. "That's it, Starling.

I've had it with you. Just leave me alone, do you hear? Take your pseudointellectual, inflated-ego self right out of my life." Starling was staring after me as I rushed up to the door. I guess I got the last word.

Starling left, as we had planned. I went to my room, changed into shorts and a T-shirt, and wandered around the silent house. I figured I'd better get used to it since neither my dad nor Starling would be around for a while.

I hate red hearts.

I also was too wound up to study, fix dinner, or stay in the house, so I grabbed my keys and, carefully locking the door behind me, got in my car and headed for the mall.

I hadn't told Starling about this part, but I hadn't known exactly when I'd go shopping. Besides, Starling was going to start watching for the watcher tonight. Nothing would happen in broad daylight at the Christiana Mall.

Still, I checked in the rearview mirror about every thirty seconds. No car was behind me for more than a few blocks at a time.

I think if someone had been following me, I'd have made a U-turn and rammed him. Can you imagine explaining that to the police when it turned out to be some innocent, unsuspecting man who just happened to live near me and just happened to be going to the mall?

Get a grip, Bethany, I lectured myself.

Besides, Starling would figure out who it was.

Somehow that thought didn't make me stop looking behind me.

Do you know how disgusting most white dresses are? I figured that since graduation is one of those formal ceremonies, I should wear a white dress. I must have seen two hundred of them that were either covered with ruffles and lace or glittering with rhinestones on some kind of tight, clingy fabric. I refused to even touch them, let alone try them on.

It's not that I hate feminine clothes, although I admit that jeans and turtlenecks or T-shirts are my favorite attire. It's just that I like things that are big and comfortable. I have no desire to display my body in some attempt to be provocative or flashy or anything.

That thought made me even more confused. Why was this guy following me? Why not one of those girls with the big hair and the miniskirt and the low-cut top? I prided myself on being just about invisible, able to blend in, not attract notice, not get involved.

Sure, Starling had noticed me, but Starling isn't exactly your normal male, either.

To begin with, he's smart and he doesn't spit.

Okay, so I was being cynical about males.

A dress for graduation. That's what I was here for. Usually it doesn't bother me at all that I don't have any female friends, but just for a moment I wished I had someone along to give me some fashion advice.

The moment passed.

A medium order of Surfside French fries renewed my determination to find a dress so I didn't have to go shopping anymore. The mall was filling up with packs of twelve-year-old girls trying to look seventeen. They really depressed me. They all chomped gum, giggled, cursed, and tried to look tough. I think they'd cornered the market on skin-tight jeans and jackets with studs on them. Didn't they know it was 89 degrees out and humid? They drifted around me in clouds of hair spray. I sure hoped nobody lit a match.

I finally bought a dress at the last place I looked. I didn't love it, but I almost liked it, which was good enough for me. It was some kind of fabric that looked like linen, and it was white with a tiny stripe of peach in it. The lines were really simple, straight and uncomplicated with no fussy details. It had a square collar and pearl buttons down the front, it was plenty big, and it cost $49.99. There. What more could someone who hated shopping ask for?

I gave the salesperson my father's money and headed for home.

I had exams to study for.

I had strange sounds to listen for.

I searched everywhere as I neared home, looking for somebody suspicious, looking for Starling. I found neither. Either Starling wasn't on duty yet, or he was slicker than I had given him credit for.

Chapter 21

I was proud of myself. I actually got some studying done, and I actually got some sleep.

It killed me the next day at school not to be able to ask Starling what had happened, where he had been, and what he had seen. I knew he must not have found the guy, because then this whole charade could end. Instead, I watched him refuse to look at me, and I didn't say a word to him.

Jyl watched us in physics with a smile on her face.

Mr. Clements forgot to ask us for a pass.

I knew most of what was on the exam, even though I worked until the last minute of class and Starling finished with half an hour to spare. Damn him and his photographic memory.

As the bell rang and I walked out of physics for the last time, Starling managed to slip a folded sheet of paper into my bookbag. Then he stomped off in one direction, and I went in the other, suddenly realizing that I was heading down the completely wrong hallway to get to my next exam.

I retraced my steps while reading the paper Starling had given me.

Valedictory Speech, Draft Two

Family, faculty, friends, and fellow members of tonight's graduating class:

Tonight, as we move into adulthood, diplomas in hand, we face a world that is in frightening disarray. The adults who have come before us, and those who are now in charge, have left us with a daunting list of problems, which we, as the future caretakers of society, must address. As we sit here tonight, I would like you to consider the challenges that await us.

We must:
save the rain forests
repair the hole in the ozone layer
buy cruelty-free products
save the whales
stop nuclear testing
recycle
watch our cholesterol
conserve energy

use a rag, not a paper towel
reduce our red meat consumption
find the children on the milk cartons
stop police brutality
boycott dolphin-killing tuna companies
lower taxes
help the homeless
rally against rape
strive for racial harmony
monitor the international balance of power
use white toilet paper with no dyes
have safe sex
stop censorship
listen to music at a safe volume
buckle up; it's the law
find a cure for AIDS
take care of our parents in their golden years
contribute to the Social Security fund
and, of course, last but not least,
just say no.

I don't know about the rest of you, but I'm exhausted already.

So, go forth into the world, remembering that commencement is not an ending, but a beginning.

Good luck.

We're all going to need it.

The only good thing about exams is that after two hour-and-a-half periods, we get to go home. I guess they figure we'll have no brains left after that, and they're about right. Luckily, Starling called me a couple of minutes after I walked in the door.

"So what do you think of my speech?" he asked.

"I love it," I said with a laugh.

"No, seriously."

"Really. I think it's great. It addresses a lot of important issues and it's short. What more do you want from a graduation speech?"

"So you think I should give it?"

"Of course you should. You might want to warn your parents, though."

"Nah," Starling said. "They've been through so much with me that they're counting down the minutes until they never can be called in to the principal's office again. I don't think they care what I say as long as I'm out of there."

"Well, after that speech I think you'll definitely be out of there," I said. "What happened last night?"

"I lurked, I melted into shadows, I surveilled, I did all those spy things."

"And?"

"And you live in a really boring neighborhood. Except, of course, for that man two houses down who, near as I could tell, dresses up in women's clothing."

"Starling!"

"Seriously, Bethany. It's either that or some weird costume party is coming up."

"Let's go with the party theory," I said. "That man goes off to work every day in a suit and tie, carrying a briefcase."

"If you had to wear a suit and tie every day, wouldn't you need to do something to break loose, too?" Starling asked.

"So you didn't find the person following me?"

"Give me time," Starling said. "It was only one night."

"Has Jyl called yet?" I asked.

"Yes," Starling admitted. "If I weren't such an honest guy, I'd have gone out with her just to further our plans."

"Great. Who do you want me to go out with?"

"Do you know any guys who are headed straight from high school into a monastery?"

"That's not fair. Jyl's not exactly a candidate for the convent."

"The prices I pay for you." Starling sighed. "I'd better go get ready for today's watching."

"How are you going to do it?" I asked.

"Professional secret. Remember, you're

going for a walk in a two-block square heading left when you leave your house. Six-thirty." With that he hung up. How dare he not tell me his plan? If I knew *where* he was going to be, I could watch for him.

I guess that's why he didn't tell me.

I walked. I didn't see anybody except some little kids that live down the street, an old lady walking an overweight cocker spaniel, and the normal cars driving by, none of which slowed down near me.

I hoped Starling would call back, but he didn't.

The only person who called was my father, double-checking on what time graduation started. I told him seven-thirty, and he said he would have to come straight there from the airport, but he'd be there. I told him I got a dress and thanked him.

Three more days of exams, then two days off while the teachers finished calculating grades and the school figured out who exactly was graduating. Then graduation day, with a rehearsal at one o'clock and the real thing that evening.

Then I'd be done with high school forever. Good.

SHE HAS MADE A SERIOUS MISTAKE.

DOES SHE THINK I AM STUPID?

DOES SHE THINK I WON'T NOTICE THAT SILLY FRIEND OF HERS TRYING TO FIGURE OUT WHO I AM?

WHY DOESN'T SHE SEE THAT I ONLY WANT WHAT NEEDS TO BE?

I WILL HAVE TO SHOW HER.

VERY SOON, I WILL HAVE TO SHOW HER.

Chapter 22

Graduation day.

Whether Starling agreed or disagreed, I had decided. This was it. The plan was off.

I was sick of not seeing Starling. I had to pretend in school that I hated his guts, and I had to watch Jyl come on to him. I had the last two days of great summer weather free of school, and I couldn't even spend them with Starling.

I was tired of watching and listening and wondering.

Besides, there hadn't been any red hearts or notes or flowers or anything for days and days. Maybe he had given up. Maybe he'd moved away. Maybe he'd found someone who wanted his attention.

Anyway, this was graduation day. I wanted to be happy. I didn't want to put on some show for a guy who probably wasn't even around anymore.

Actually, I was even more angry at this person than usual. If he was going to leave me alone now, why didn't he at least have the courtesy to tell me so I could stop worrying about him? One last note would be great: *Dear Bethany, I've tossed you aside for a long-legged blonde with big hair. Sorry.*

I'd celebrate.

But I was going to celebrate anyway. I was going to call Starling and tell him that I wanted a ride to graduation practice, and that his spying days were over no matter what he said. Somehow I didn't think he'd complain too much. The novelty must be wearing off, even for someone as inventive as Starling.

Actually, I was kind of proud of him. I hadn't heard of any police reports being filed by neighbors complaining about a Peeping Tom or a suspicious character loitering in the bushes. He must have done a pretty good job of hiding himself after all.

I just hoped he hadn't been inspired by the man down the street and done part of his spying in women's clothing.

I stretched out in bed, luxuriating in the fact that I didn't have to rush off to school or anywhere else. No more high school. It was taking a while for that to sink in. Sure, there was college for the next four years, but that was different.

No more teachers watching your every move.

No more hall passes, bathroom passes, morning announcements, pep fests, petty little cliques.

I'd never have to say the Pledge of Allegiance again.

I looked at the clock beside my bed. It was ten o'clock already. No problem. Rehearsal was at one o'clock, so I still had plenty of time to shower, eat breakfast, call Starling, and get to rehearsal. Then maybe we could go out for a late lunch. I'd even treat, to thank him for all the time he'd spent trying to find the red heart jerk.

I'd gone to bed in my favorite summertime clothes: a men's triple-extra-large T-shirt. They're great. They come almost to the knee, and they're huge and baggy and cool. Under it, although they didn't show, I had on a pair of white boxer shorts.

I laughed as I headed for the bathroom. I'd better change before I went to rehearsal or Starling would claim that now I was cross-dressing.

I headed immediately for my toothbrush. I

hate that morning-mouth feeling. My hand froze before it made it to my toothbrush, though.

There on the bathroom mirror was a red heart.

I closed my eyes and rubbed them, my heart racing. I had to be seeing things. That had to be some kind of bizarre reflection, the sun shining off the silver faucet or something. It wouldn't be there when I looked again. It couldn't be.

It was.

One red heart was pasted right in the middle of the mirror. I reached out as if I were hypnotized and rubbed my finger over its surface. I felt the edge where it met the glass.

There was a red heart on the bathroom mirror.

It hadn't been there last night. I would have noticed, wouldn't I?

Of course I would have.

Maybe my father had come home in the middle of the night and pasted that heart there.

My father was in California.

There were no good excuses, no conclusions to arrive at other than the one I was so desperately trying to avoid.

He had been here, in my house, in my bathroom.

When?

Was he still here?

I listened more intently than I've ever listened in my life, frozen in place as if I'd never move again. Maybe if I didn't move, didn't breathe, he wouldn't know I was here.

Maybe he was already gone.

If he wasn't, maybe he'd leave.

No, I'd leave. I suddenly knew that I had to get out of the house. I couldn't just stand there in the bathroom. If he were gone, I had to find out how he'd gotten in, and how to keep him out. If he were still here, I had to get away from him.

I had to go to the police. I had to make them believe me this time.

No, I had to go to Starling. Then I'd go to the police.

The phone was in the hallway. I could call Starling. I could call 911. Then I could barricade myself in my room and wait for someone to come help me.

Or I could run now, run as fast as I could, get away from that red heart and then call somebody.

My mind whirled in circles. Call. Run. Red hearts.

Then I heard a noise. It sounded like someone was on the stairs. There's one about three up from the bottom that always squeaks. That was what I had heard.

Or was it? Maybe it was my imagination. He must be gone. He had to be gone. Didn't he?

Then inspiration hit. Sometimes when Starling and I were talking and I didn't want to be overheard by my father, I'd take the phone into my room. The cord was just long enough for me to pull it a few feet into my room, where I'd lay on the floor and talk in privacy. That was what I'd do. I'd take the phone into my room, then barricade the door with my dresser, and then call the police and Starling.

Now all I had to do was convince my feet to move. If he was on the steps, he'd see me. There was no way around that. Still, all I had to do was snag the phone and lunge into my room and slam the door.

What if he wasn't there, and I called the police and they thought I was an idiot? Too bad. At least I could make them search the house and figure out how he'd gotten in. Plus I could call Starling. Maybe he could meet the police here and fill them in.

I had to move. I wiggled my toes, just to make sure that my body was capable of movement.

I wanted to stay where I was. But I wanted the phone worse.

I took three deep breaths and bolted for the phone. I burst through the bathroom door, refusing to look toward the stairs, my full attention on the phone on the wooden stand in the hallway. There it was, a simple beige instrument that held all the answers. In three steps I was there, and my shaking hand grabbed the phone, my eyes already glued to my open bedroom door which was my next destination.

I was almost to the door, almost ready to dash through the door and throw it shut, when two facts registered simultaneously. First, the phone seemed to be coming with me with no resistance, no tangling of the long cord. When I desperately looked down, I saw why.

The cord had been cut.

Then I saw motion in my bedroom.

Somebody was in there.

I didn't wait long enough to get a better look. I only knew that there was someone there, standing beside my bed in front of the window. The bright summer sun was streaming in, leaving me more an outline than features, but I knew that this was not my imagination.

I dropped the phone and headed for the steps.

No way was I staying here. I flew down the steps, missing some, lunging awkwardly down. I hit the bottom on the run, headed for the front door.

Chain, deadbolt, doorknob lock. All were on. I fumbled with them.

"Bethany, wait." A quiet voice behind me, footsteps coming down the stairs, not rushing, just methodical.

Don't look. Don't listen. Just get these locks undone and get out of here.

I got the chain off and turned the deadbolt.

"Don't run, Bethany. We need to talk."

Sure. You break into my house, scare me to death, and you want to talk? Well, you can just keep talking, but I'm out of here.

My panicky fingers turned the lock on the doorknob and I wrenched open the door, half expecting it not to open.

It did, and I almost cried in relief.

"You can't run away from me, Bethany," said that same quiet voice, this time much closer.

Watch me, I thought.

I was out the door. The outside world looked deceptively normal. Sunshine, birds, hot steps against my bare feet. I was off at a run. I didn't know where I was going, but I was getting as far away from here as I could.

Far enough to get help.

Far enough to get to a phone.

Somebody had to be home. Somebody had to let me in and lock the door safely behind me. I looked longingly at my car sitting in the driveway. Of course I had locked the car doors, and of course I didn't have my keys.

Okay. I'd find another way. Who would be home?

I ran across the front yard and toward the neighbor's house, desperately trying to think if anybody would be home. No. They both worked, and they left about the same time I normally left for school. I dashed through their front yard, headed for the next house. There were bushes at the property line, and I pushed through them, only vaguely aware of the thorns scratching me.

There was a car in the driveway. Somebody must be there. I raced up to the front door and pounded on it, searched for a doorbell, found a button, pushed it frantically.

Over the noise I heard the soft thud of running footsteps. They stopped as I whirled around, my finger still on the doorbell.

He was about six feet tall with close-cut dark hair, jeans, and a black T-shirt. He was actually good-looking, not at all demented-looking or disfigured or anything.

He had broken into my house.

He had cut the phone cord.

And he was about to say something. "Bethany, you can't get away from me."

With one last frustrated thud on the door, I took off, hurtling off the far side of the steps. This time I cut through the side yard and into the backyard, desperately searching for something that would hide me from his sight. My heart was pounding so hard that I thought I'd have a heart attack.

My mind turned briefly to Mr. Baldwin. Maybe we'd have the same heart doctor.

Mr. Baldwin. Maybe I could get as far as his house. He'd be home, or else he'd be out walking Wolfgang. Either way I could get help.

Then a glimmer of logic shone through my panic. Mr. Baldwin lived at least ten or twelve miles away. I remember in gym when we had to run a mile and I felt like I'd die. How could I run ten or twelve?

Considering the options, maybe I'd have to try.

I was too afraid to turn around, afraid of what I'd see. I kept running, cursing my neighbors for having such tidy yards, cursing them for not being home, cursing them for not noticing me running through their yards with some lunatic following me.

I made it to the next street before I heard the voice again.

"Bethany, this won't work. Stop and talk to me."

He didn't even sound winded while I was panting, desperately fighting for each gulp of air. I ran into the middle of the street, not caring that he could see me. It was mid-morning in a suburban neighborhood. It wasn't like I lived out in the boondocks somewhere. There had to be cars. And when I saw one, I'd throw myself at it to make it stop.

I pounded down the street, the rough pavement cutting into my bare feet, rocks and glass and pain. I barely felt it. Air. I needed to breathe. I needed to stop running.

I couldn't.

"Bethany," I heard him say. I whirled around, and he was no more than ten feet behind me, running easily. He didn't even seem to be trying hard, almost like he was playing with me, keeping me within reach.

A burst of anger filled me. I desperately looked for cars and saw none. I headed over the curb, racing toward another house, another door. I couldn't stand being so clearly in sight.

A sob tore from me as I pounded on the door; then, when he started through the yard,

I stumbled off the step and around the house. At the back there was a garage.

I ran for it, grabbed the doorknob, and turned.

The door opened. Blessing the owner who was trusting or careless enough to leave his garage unlocked, I threw myself inside, gasping for air and searching for help.

If I couldn't hide, maybe I could find a weapon, something to keep him away from me.

There wasn't a car in the garage, and the biggest thing in it was a lawnmower. So much for hiding.

Hanging on a pegboard were gardening tools, screwdrivers, some extension cords.

Leaning in the corner was a shovel. Sobbing with fear and frustration, I reached for the shovel. Just as my hand closed over the wooden handle, he was there.

His hand clamped over mine, and his breath was hot against my tear-damp cheek.

"Good job, Bethany. We're almost there."

I was at the end of my endurance, my lungs aching, my legs shaking. I didn't think I could run again.

Instead, I tried to wrench my hand free and grab the shovel and swing. He grabbed my wrist, and this time he clamped down hard enough to hurt.

"Come with me, Bethany. You have no choice."

At the moment, I couldn't figure out what choices I had, but going with him wasn't one of them. I refused to move. The longer I stood there, the more time I had to get ready for another dash. Besides, maybe somebody would come along. Maybe the owner of this garage would pull into his driveway. Imagine his surprise.

Imagine my gratitude.

There were no sounds other than my gasps and his quiet, calm breathing. I readied myself for the next round. Maybe I could step on his foot, throw him off balance, and spin away from him.

Bare feet don't work well at inflicting pain on feet wearing shoes. I tried it anyway.

"We're almost there," he whispered. "Come with me."

He never let go of my wrist, but rather pulled it behind me. Any way I struggled brought pain.

"Walk beside me."

He half-dragged, half-wrenched me out of the garage and through the backyard. As soon as we were outside again, I screamed for help.

"Nice thing about suburban neighborhoods," he said conversationally. "Everybody's either at work or minding his own business."

I struggled until my arm felt dislocated, but still we were moving through the yard, then the next one. My cries were mocked by the birds that chirped innocently in the trees.

As I screamed, he laughed, loud and joyously. "You're such a tease," he called out once when a car drove near.

Either the driver didn't hear us because of the distance between the street and the backyard, or the driver didn't care, or he thought we were just silly kids playing around.

I lost track of where we were as I fought and screamed. I don't think we were more than four or five houses down the street when he turned me toward the back door of a small brick house. The grass in the yard was taller than the neighboring yards, and all of the blinds were drawn.

He pushed open the door and walked me in. The door shut behind me, and I heard him turn the locks.

"Now we can talk," he said.

Right. There had to be another way out of here. As soon as I caught my breath, I'd find it.

In the meantime I looked around, trying to get a sense of the layout of the house. We were in a kitchen with a small wooden table and four chairs, bare countertops, an old refrigerator. Although it was clean, it looked unused, smelled closed up. Through the doorway I could see into the dining room with a big dining room table with old-fashioned wooden chairs with fancy carved backs. On the table was one of those fake plastic flower arrangements.

Whose house was this?

I cursed the fact that my father and I had made absolutely no effort to get to know the neighbors beyond those to either side. We were so used to moving all the time that neither of us invested much time or energy in casual acquaintances.

Now I was only a few streets from home, maybe four blocks, and I couldn't place the house or who might live in it. Actually, it had the feel of a place whose owners were away for a long time.

Or maybe they were dead.

Chapter 23

"Let's go into the living room and sit down, Bethany," he said quietly, calmly. "We need to talk."

Sure. No problem. You break into my house, chase me all over the neighborhood, force me to come here, and now we'll just chat. I half expected him to offer me a cup of tea.

Still, when he started out of the kitchen, I followed him. I wanted to see more of the house so I could figure out the best way out of there.

The living room had a matching sofa and chair covered with a brown, worn, nubby fabric. Small tables dotted the room, and a big, old television built into a cabinet was in one corner. The whole place looked old. There were wide, dusty venetian blinds that fully covered the front windows, and a large wooden door that had a chain lock on it. I calculated how long it would take me to get there and get it open and get out.

What then, though? He'd outrun me before, and I supposed he would do it again. I needed a better plan. I needed to time it so that more people were around.

Or I needed to slow him down.

Or stop him.

I looked around the room with a new perspective. There was a lamp on the table at the end of the sofa, and several dusty ceramic birds. Another table held some volumes of those *Reader's Digest* condensed books.

"Sit down, Bethany."

I sat on the very edge of the sofa on the end next to the table with the lamp.

"I'm sorry that you made this so difficult."

I realized that I had not yet said a word. Maybe it was time. I needed some time to recover, some time to figure out a plan.

"Why are you doing this?" I asked.

"I've told you why in my notes," he said.

I studied his face. Under other circumstances I might have thought he was good-looking. His teeth were straight and white, his nose strong. His eyes were dark, his hair thick, even though it was cropped short.

"I still don't understand," I said.

"We are meant to be together," he said.

"Why?" I asked. "How do you know this?"

"I believe that for every person, there is one other person who is fated to be his completion, the answer to all that he needs. You are that person for me."

I stopped the first words that came to my mind, which were, "Are you crazy?" I didn't need to antagonize him. Instead, I said, "How do you know that I am this person?"

"It is the way that I felt the first moment that I truly saw you. I felt relief. I believed for the first time that I might not have to live forever in loneliness. You are the answer."

What the hell was he talking about? All of this might be interesting if I weren't basically his hostage in some stuffy house. I tried to choose my words carefully. "I'm not sure that I have the answers for much of anything."

"But you do," he said calmly. "You are perfect."

I laughed. I couldn't help it. I've been accused of many traits, but being perfect was sure not one of them. I wished Starling were here to hear this.

I wished Starling were here, period.

I stopped laughing and looked him dead in the face. "I am not perfect."

"You are. You are everything that I am not."

Like sane, maybe, I thought. Still, I needed

to understand this. Maybe it would help me to get away from him.

"What am I?" I asked. "What do you see in me?"

"You are beautiful."

Well, that was a nice start, but I'd take being free of him over being complimented by him.

"You are in control, and successful. You are moving forward."

Sure, except when I'm running in circles trying to get away from you, I thought, gazing longingly at the door.

He must have seen my look. "Please don't try to leave," he said. "You must stay with me. You must come to understand that you are the answer, that you must be with me. You are the only one who can save me."

"Save you from what?"

"From despair. From myself."

Great. Did this guy always talk in riddles? I needed some more answers.

"What despair?"

"I have failed," he said.

"Who hasn't?" I said.

"You haven't," he said.

"Of course I have," I said.

"At what?"

"I failed a history paper," I said, my mind racing. Of course, that had been part of a plot on Mr. Baldwin's part, but I didn't want to go into that. Mr. Baldwin. What I wouldn't give to see his grumpy face right about now.

"See what I mean? You have never failed at anything of significance. You couldn't."

"And you have?"

I needed to keep him talking so that I could use the time to come up with a plan. What would Starling do?

"I have failed at everything. Everything except finding you."

"Somehow I doubt that. What have you failed at?"

"I can't tell you that. Then you will look at me the way others do. With contempt. With pity."

How about with fear and hatred? "No, I won't," I said. "Tell me what you've failed at."

"Chemistry."

Chemistry? I looked at him in complete disbelief. This guy had gone off the deep end and kidnapped me because he had failed *chemistry?* This was absolutely absurd. In fact, it was so stupid that it made me mad.

"You failed chemistry. Big deal. I bet about a quarter of the class did."

"You don't understand."

Well, at least he knew I wasn't perfect anymore. Maybe he'd let me go and find somebody more sympathetic. "Look, lots of people fail science classes. It doesn't mean that they're bad people or have ruined their lives or anything."

"That's exactly what it means."

"Why?" I asked. "So take it again. Take a different class."

"I can't."

I looked at him more closely. He seemed to be about my age, maybe a little bit older. "Where do you go to school?" I asked.

"University of Delaware," he answered.

"That explains it," I said, feeling on more stable ground. "The University of Delaware is famous for its chemical engineering program, so its chemistry department is full of tough professors. You could always change your major, or go to another school or something."

"It's not engineering."

"So get completely away from that field," I reasoned. "Be an English major or something."

"That would be impossible," he said.

"Why?" I asked. I couldn't believe he was making such a big deal of this.

"I have to get into medical school, and I'll never get in with an F in chemistry."

"So don't go to medical school." I was losing

patience with him. "There are a million other things you could be."

"There is nothing else I could be," he said, his voice tense.

"You mean that you believe you are meant to be a doctor and nothing else?" I said, trying to understand. Maybe he was filled with all these absolute certainties: He had to be a doctor; he had to have me. Very strange.

"No." So much for that theory. "I am expected to be one."

Now that made some sense. "You mean your parents want you to be a doctor?"

"*Want* doesn't describe it. From the time I was a child, that's all they've talked about."

"They'll get over it," I said. "Maybe they'll be disappointed for a little while, but once they see you're happy doing something you're good at, they'll be fine."

"No, they won't," he said with absolute certainty.

"Give them a chance. You're their son. They must love you."

As soon as I said the words, I knew I might be wrong, but I couldn't take them back.

"They love their son the doctor, the one who got such good grades in high school, the one who's in premed, the one who's going to be a doctor and make them proud." His voice was filled with such bitterness that I looked at him, my full attention on him.

"Then forget about what they want," I said softly. "You can't live your life to please them. You owe it to yourself to find what you want."

"I can't live as a failure."

I tried to reason with him. "You're only a failure at one silly course. That doesn't make you a failure at life."

"Yes, it does. I will be nothing but a disappointment. Every time they look at me, they will see what I'm not."

"That's their problem."

"But it's my problem, too," he said. "There's only one answer."

"What's that?"

"You."

I was afraid of that. "How am I the answer?"

"If I can prove that I am worthy of you, then I can prove that I'm not a failure."

Okay, how out of touch with reality was this guy? What if I agreed with him? What if I said, "Fine. Let's go meet Mom and Dad, let them see how perfect I am?" Would he take me? I'd sure have an opportunity to get away, to get help.

"Do you want me to meet your parents?" I asked cautiously.

"Yes," he said.

I breathed a sigh of relief. This was the answer. Once I got out of this house, the odds of screaming for help or getting away increased dramatically. "Okay," I said.

"But not yet," he said, looking at me very seriously. He must have seen the disappointment that flooded me. "First I have to prove to you how much I care about you. I have to show you that I would never hurt you, that I am meant to honor you and love you and prove myself worthy of someone like you."

"If you want to prove that you care about me, you can start by letting me go," I said. "If you want me to trust you, you have to let me spend time with you freely and willingly."

His eyes seemed to get darker. "That wouldn't work. I tried to get you to come to me, but you wouldn't. Not without him."

"That was all a mix-up," I explained. "Starling wasn't meant to follow me from the library. I hadn't told him anything."

"But he has been watching for me — I know that you don't trust me. I sent you roses and notes, but you didn't believe me."

Okay, now what? My mind was whirling in confusion. What was the key to his mind? What would make him let me go?

"I was confused," I confessed. Sort of.

"You wanted him, not me."

Starling. "He's a very good friend."

"He's more than a friend."

My anger flared up again. How long had he been watching me? "Look, Starling and I have been through a lot together. We understand each other."

"And now you need time to understand me."

That would take a lot of time, I thought. "It will take time for me to get to know you," I finally mustered up the courage to say.

"Yes," he agreed. "That is why you have to come away with me. We need to be alone. Just the two of us."

Chapter 24

"That's impossible," I said firmly, hoping my fear didn't show.

"Don't say that." His voice became very soft — almost gentle.

"I can't go away with you. People will notice I'm gone. They'll come after me." They'd better come after me, I thought.

"They'll never find us."

I didn't like the sound of this one little bit. "Look, it just won't work. My father spent his career in the Army. He'll find me if he has to tear apart the whole East Coast." I'm sure the certainty could be heard in my voice because I really believed what I was saying. My father *would* find me. Suddenly I wished I had told him a lot more than I had. But if I was missing, Starling would certainly tell my father.

"I have a very special place I know that is perfect for us," he said calmly.

"It's impossible," I said. "Look. I graduate tonight. I'm supposed to be at rehearsal this afternoon. I have to be there, or people will start looking for me."

"You mean Starling will. Your father isn't home."

Damn him. He sure had been keeping a close eye on me. "Starling will tell others." I hoped I was right.

"But we'll have a head start. It will be my graduation gift to you, Bethany. It's beautiful there, quiet and peaceful. You'll learn to love it as much as I do."

"If you want to give me a graduation gift, then let me go to graduation," I said, not liking the distant look in his eyes.

"I'm afraid that would be impossible. You might not come back to me. I can't stand to think about that."

"I'll come back," I promised, trying to sound convincing. "Just let me go to graduation."

"I'll make it up to you, Bethany. I'll give you roses and poems, and long walks at sunrise. I'll make you happy."

"I want to go now." I knew I sounded about five years old, but I couldn't help it. Suddenly this was all too much. I was tired and scared and angry. I needed to go home.

"I'm sorry you feel that way."

"This isn't going to work." I was yelling now. "Someone will find me, and then you'll be in a lot of trouble. Just let me go now before anybody else is involved."

"You really don't understand, do you?"

"No, I *don't* understand, and I *don't* want to be here, and I'm not perfect, and I just want to go home."

"I wish I could let you do that, but I can't."

"Fine. I'm out of here." I pushed myself up off the sofa and headed for the door. Maybe, just maybe, I could get out of there before he did anything.

"Bethany, you can't."

"I'm really sorry, but I have to go now. This has gone far enough."

I made it to the door and was fumbling with the chain when he grabbed me. He didn't hold my wrists hard enough to really hurt, but my yanking gained me nothing.

"I want to go," I pleaded. "I want to see my father, and I want to go to my own graduation." I was near tears. "Didn't you get to go to your graduation? Did somebody stop you?"

"Come with me," he said.

He let go of my wrists, but grabbed one arm firmly. He led me back through the living room to the stairs that went upstairs. I was completely torn. I didn't want to get any farther away from the door than I was, yet I wanted to know if there were any other escape routes. Maybe one of the windows wasn't covered. Maybe I could get out one of them. But before I could come to any conclusions, it was too late. He had guided me up the stairs to the first door on the right. He opened it, and I looked around in amazement.

The other parts of the house that I'd seen seemed old, with furniture that seemed to have been around for fifty years. This room was a boy's room. There was a brown-and-rust-plaid bedspread on a single bed, and bookshelves filled with books. I looked at the titles — *Hardy Boys*, books on snakes and dinosaurs, some science fiction. There was a small desk, and on it sat a framed graduation picture.

It was him. His hair was longer and he was smiling, but it was definitely him.

And he was wearing the graduation colors of my school.

"You went to the same high school?" I asked in surprise. He had let go of my arm, but he was still standing very close.

"You don't remember me, do you?" he asked.

"No," I admitted.

"I graduated last year," he said. "Sometimes I think that was the last time I was happy."

There were a couple of photographs on the desk, and I picked them up. He was wearing his cap and gown, and his arm was around an older woman who was beaming up at him.

"Who's that?" I asked.

"My grandmother," he said, taking the picture away from me and staring at it intently.

"She looks proud of you."

"She was. She was proud of me no matter what."

"So you don't have anything to prove to her."

His expression softened. "She died six months ago."

That explained some of this. "Was this her house?" I asked.

"Yes," he answered. "I stayed with her a lot. Most of the happy parts of my childhood were spent here."

"You must really miss her," I said.

"She loved me."

I picked up a second picture. This time he was flanked by a man and a woman.

"Your parents?" I asked.

This time he grabbed the picture from me more forcefully. I thought he was going to rip the picture, but instead he pulled open the middle desk drawer and threw it in there, slamming it shut. "Yes."

"They looked happy," I said, not sure of what to say but knowing that I should say something.

"Do you know what they said to me? 'Just think how proud we would have been if you'd been valedictorian.' I graduated second in my class, but that wasn't good enough for them."

"But that's ridiculous. Second in the class is wonderful."

"It's not good enough." His words were suddenly angry, almost hateful.

One more piece of paper was on the desk, and I reached for it, half-expecting him to snatch it away before I could look at it. It was an official computer form with the seal of the University of Delaware on it.

I studied it quickly. Second-semester grades. Freshman English, A. American History, A. Calculus, A. Conversational French, A. Chemistry, F.

"Four A's," I marveled.

"An F," he said flatly.

"You got an A in calculus and in all of these other difficult courses. You are obviously a good student, but science isn't your strong point. Study something else."

"I've already explained that," he said impatiently. "I've let them down before. I was always second best. Now I've lost my chance at med school. I can't tell them. I can't face them."

"Can't you take the course over again?"

"That wouldn't be good enough."

"Look," I said, trying to be diplomatic, "you might have to pick a different career. I think your parents will understand that. Maybe it will take them a little time to adjust, but . . ."

"Ever since I've been a little kid, my parents have bragged about how I'll be the first doctor in the family. At every family reunion, they told everybody about how they had sacrificed their whole lives to save up the money to send me to med school so that their son could have the life that they didn't. They're counting on me."

"Well, now they can spend your medical school money on a great vacation or something." I didn't mean to be flippant, but I guess it sounded that way.

"This isn't some joke," he snapped. "They've spent nineteen years building this dream, and now I'm going to destroy it."

"Look," I said, struggling around the words that I'd begun to search for before. "Your parents might be upset, but they'll adjust to the idea of your not being a doctor. I think it will be a lot harder on them if you get in trouble because of me."

"You won't get me in trouble," he replied.

Just watch me, I thought. If I get away from here, the police are going to be after you in a heartbeat. Still, I'd better not tell him that. I just wanted to convince him that if he let me go, I'd forget all about this. Then maybe I stood a chance of getting free.

I looked around the room more carefully. There were framed awards and certificates everywhere: National Honor Society, National Merit Scholar, Academic Achievement awards, all proudly displayed.

I thought it was interesting that they were all in his room at his grandmother's house, rather than at his parents' house. Weren't these awards good enough for his parents, either?

I looked at them again: Brent Powell.

I vaguely remembered the name. I'd heard it on intercom announcements, maybe, or seen it in the school newspaper. Except, of course, for Starling and Jyl and a few others, I really didn't pay much attention to the people in my own class, let alone those a year ahead of me.

Jyl. What if I disappeared? Would she be there to fill in for me?

Stop it. I had to get a grip. He was speaking to me again.

"Do you remember me now?" he asked, still staying very close to me.

"I remember hearing your name for awards and things." Then I added, "I really don't get involved in school very much."

"I know." He smiled. "That's part of what makes you special. You're not one of those empty-headed cheerleaders or those stupid girls that spend all their time combing their hair and shopping."

Well, he was right about that part.

"How did you notice me?" I guess that still really bothered me. Why me? I wanted an honest answer, not that stuff about how we were two parts of one whole. "*Where* did you notice me?" I asked, changing my question to make it more specific.

"I had to go back to get a letter of recommendation and I was walking down the hallway when classes were changing. You were coming down the hall, and even though there were hundreds of people around, it was like there was a space around you that set you off from everyone else."

It was probably the fact that, other than Starling, I really didn't have friends at school so I was by myself. A rather simple explanation.

"I remembered seeing you around during my senior year, but I don't think I really saw you until that day. You looked at me, and it was like you could see right through me and into my heart."

Great. He thought I was looking into his heart, and I didn't even remember ever seeing him.

"I realized how beautiful your eyes were, and how natural the glow was that radiated from you."

I was probably mad at Starling or thinking about physics or something, and he thought I was glowing.

"How did you find out who I was?" I asked, refusing to listen to any more.

"I found your picture in the yearbook," he said.

Right. That was really hard. I should have figured that one out myself.

"How did you find out my locker combination?"

"I stood near you one day. I actually saw you many times in school before I dared to communicate with you."

"And then you followed me?"

"I had to, Bethany. I had to be near you. I

had to find a way to make you know how important you are to me. I felt like I was drowning, and you were the only one who could save me."

He really wasn't in touch with reality. How could I break through to him?

"Brent," I began.

"I hope you'll forgive me for what I have to do next," he said.

I whirled to look at him.

He was holding a piece of rope.

Chapter 25

"No," I pleaded. "Don't."

"I'm sorry, Bethany," he said, coming toward me as I edged for the door.

"You can't do this to me if you say you care about me," I said desperately.

"I'm doing this because I do care about you," he said. "It's only for a little while, just so I can go and get the supplies that we'll need to go away."

"I'm not going away with you," I said fiercely.

"That's why I have to do this. You don't believe me yet. You don't trust me yet. I have to take you away to prove how much I care about you. But until then, I can't trust that you'll wait for me."

"I'll wait," I promised, but I guess he saw through my lie. I made a run for it then, dashed for the door, ready for any attempt that would get me away from that rope.

He had me before I got through the door. He pushed me onto the bed and tied my wrists together while I struggled and screamed and kicked. I desperately tried to remember what I should do to make it possible to get free, but all I could do was try to get free of him.

I made it difficult, but he succeeded. My wrists were tied together and to one of the headposts; my ankles were tied to a post at the bottom of the bed. The whole time I screamed and threatened and pleaded. Finally, exhausted, petrified, I quieted myself.

Once he left, maybe I could figure out a way to get free.

"I'll be back just as soon as I can," he promised. "Please don't hate me for this. I just have to keep you here until we can leave. I'll make it up to you. I promise I will. I'm only doing this because I care about you and need you."

I glared at him, gasping for breath.

"I'll make it up to you," he repeated.

At least he hadn't gagged me. I figured that as soon as he left, I'd scream until somebody had to hear me. There were houses nearby. Eventually somebody would come home or turn off the television or take out the trash or *something* and hear me. I listened as he went down the stairs.

I wondered if he knew that if I had anything to do with it, he'd sure not find me here when he came back. I'd be at home. I'd be at the police station. I'd be with Starling. I'd be anywhere but here.

I heard his footsteps downstairs, and then I came to know why he hadn't gagged me. He turned on the television set downstairs in the living room. Loud. So loud that I'd have a hard time being heard over it.

Well, maybe somebody would be suspicious about the loud television.

Loud enough to call the police?

I waited a few minutes until I figured he was gone, even though I couldn't hear him leave over the din of the television. It sounded like some old western was on, lots of shouting and shooting. Great.

I waited until a commercial came on, and I screamed for help. I had heard somewhere that more people respond to a cry of fire than a cry for help, so I screamed fire. I screamed that I was being held there against my will, and for somebody to call the police. I screamed until my voice was hoarse and my throat ached.

All I heard was the television.

I struggled against the ropes. I tried to remember how people in the movies and on television always got free when they were tied up. It seemed like they always maneuvered one hand free or rubbed the rope against the edge of something. I tried, but the ropes were so secure that the only thing that gave was my flesh. I twisted and turned against the ropes until my wrists and ankles were raw. I thought maybe the blood would help me slip free of the ropes, but it didn't.

I screamed in fear and frustration and anger and pain.

It was a nightmare. Time passed in slow motion, a lot of time. My wrists and ankles throbbed and burned. I tried to figure out a new plan. I still screamed when there were lulls in the television sound, but my voice was so hoarse now that I knew I stood no chance of being heard.

I needed a plan, but I was tired.

Tired and scared.

But part of me was also very angry. This was my graduation day. I wasn't sure what time it was, but I undoubtedly had missed the rehearsal by now. What would my father think when he rushed to school from the airport to see me graduate, and I wasn't there?

My father. And Starling. Those two

thoughts kept me sane. After all, if I didn't show up at practice, Starling would know that something was up.

The question was, what could he do? Could he go to the police? If he went to my house, he'd find the front door unlocked, which he would know was unusual for me, but was that enough to get the police to look for me?

Considering our experience at the police station, I doubted that.

I tried to think of what might possibly lead Starling to this house. What would make him suspicious?

I suddenly thought of all the things I should have done. On television the person being kidnapped always has the presence of mind to leave the ring that never leaves her finger on the ground, or to write the name of the kidnapper in blood on the wall before she's taken away or something.

What had I left to help Starling find me? Nothing. I don't wear any special jewelry, and I hadn't had anything with me to leave behind even if I had thought to do so. I had on white boxer shorts and a white T-shirt, no shoes, no jewelry, nothing else. I didn't exactly have many choices of something to leave behind.

Still, I should have thought of a way to lead Starling to me.

I decided that if I died and they made a movie of the week about this, it wouldn't make a very good story.

If I died. Now there was a thought that I needed to avoid dwelling on.

Funny, through all of this I really hadn't thought that he might kill me.

But he might. He certainly was depressed and angry and feeling hopeless.

And fixated on me as the answer.

What would happen when he found out that I wasn't the answer? When he found out that I didn't even have any answers for myself, let alone for him?

I needed a plan before he got back.

Get him to untie me and then leap out the window?

Bash him over the head with one of his trophies?

Overpower him and tie him up just like he'd tied me?

I needed to get free so that I could get out of here, but my bleeding wrists and ankles seemed to have swollen, if anything, and the ropes were tighter than ever.

The television suddenly went silent.

For a moment, I hoped that this was a break, that the television had blown up or overheated or something.

Then I heard his footsteps on the stairs.

He looked at me sadly. I'm sure that I wasn't a very pretty sight.

"I tried to hurry," he said, coming over to sit beside me on the bed. "I didn't know what foods you liked or what size clothes you wore or anything, so I had to get more than I thought. I didn't want you to do without anything while we're away."

"I have to go to the bathroom."

That was about as far as my plan had gotten. I needed to get him to untie me, and, in all honesty, I did need to go to the bathroom.

"I'm sorry," he whispered, but he made no move to untie me.

"If you ever want me to trust you, you have to treat me with enough decency to let me go to the bathroom," I said firmly. "If you don't, if you degrade me, I'll never believe that you care about me."

"You won't try to run?"

"No." Actually, I wasn't sure that I could. I needed to test my legs, to see if I actually was capable of the burst of speed that I'd need. My ankles hurt fiercely, and he must have noticed the blood and the hoarseness in my voice.

He had no reason to believe me, but what was he going to do?

I almost felt grateful when he untied my ankles, then my wrists. Almost.

I moved to sit on the edge of the bed, dizzy at first. Still, I felt like anything was possible now that I was freed of those ropes. Maybe there was a window in the bathroom.

There wasn't. He walked me there, and he refused to let me shut the door. The door opened outward, and he stood against it.

At least, as he had promised, he didn't look in. I ran water and used a towel hanging in the bathroom to clean some of the blood off my wrists and ankles. I flexed my ankles. They hurt, but they moved. When I flushed the toilet, I used the noise as a cover for opening the medicine cabinet. I don't know what I was looking for — anything that might help me. A razor. Glass. Something that I could hide to use as a weapon.

It was completely empty except for a plastic bottle half-filled with antacid tablets. I couldn't figure out any use for them.

I'd delayed long enough.

I walked out the door, hoping he wouldn't be there, hoping I could get down the steps.

He was waiting for me. "We need to leave now."

I didn't like the sound of that. If we left, that would make it harder for Starling or my father or the police to find me. On the other hand, while we were leaving or while we were in the car, maybe I could find a way to get free.

"Can we talk about this for a minute?" I asked.

He looked puzzled, but he agreed, escorting me back to the bedroom that his grandmother had so lovingly filled with the evidence of his successes.

What a shame that those successes had never been enough.

I sat down on the chair that was pulled up to the desk, and he paced before me. There was no way I was getting near that bed again. I could see the bloodstains on the bedspread.

"Sit down for a minute," I suggested.

He sat at the foot of the bed, close to me, too close to run for it.

"Tell me again why we need to go away," I said, looking at him, searching his face, looking for a way into his mind.

"I can't stand it here any longer. I can't stand to be here when my parents see my grades, when they know for sure that I'm a failure, that I'll never be what they want."

He was deadly serious. There was no hiding the pain that this prospect brought to him.

"Why don't you go alone?" I asked. "Why

don't you use the time to be alone and think everything through? That way you can decide what you want, what kind of future you need to make you happy."

"No!" he screamed, leaning toward me and grabbing my wrists. He let go again when I flinched from the contact on my bruised and bleeding skin. "I can't do it alone."

"Of course you can. People do their very best thinking when they're alone."

"No!" he repeated. "I can't. I *need* you there with me."

"I'm not the answer," I said, my voice hoarse and rough. "There *are* answers, but they're inside of you. You have to find them for yourself."

He put his head in his hands. "You don't understand."

"Then explain it to me," I said.

And he did.

He told me about his older brother Justin, who had died of bone cancer when he was seven. It was Justin, according to the stories he had heard all of his life, who was brilliant, who could read when he was three, and who amazed his doctors at five and six and seven by asking all kinds of medical questions and seeming to understand all of their answers. It was Justin whose funeral was attended by all the doctors who had treated him, and it was the doctors who said that, had he lived, Justin would have been one of them.

It was Justin whose death had almost killed his mother.

And he was the one who had been born on the second anniversary of Justin's death. His mother took it as a sign that he was meant to carry on Justin's spirit, Justin's life. They spent part of every birthday at the cemetery.

But he never had measured up.

When he couldn't read at three, his mother had taken him to be tested. She wasn't satisfied to hear that he was developmentally normal, and that he would read in a few years when he was ready. She hired special tutors.

When he went to kindergarten and preferred playing with the other kids rather than learning his shapes and colors, she punished him.

When he didn't test high enough for the elementary school gifted program, his mother went to school and demanded that he be placed in it anyway. After being threatened with a lawsuit, the school agreed.

He was smart, a good student, a fine athlete. But it wasn't enough. He wasn't first. Justin would have been. He wasn't naturally gifted in math and science. Justin was.

After a while, his mother didn't even have to mention Justin. He knew what she was thinking when he brought home a report card with all A's except for one B, and she honestly tried to say that it was okay.

It wasn't. She didn't have to say it. He could see it in her eyes.

His father tried to help, but he, too, faced his sorrows at the death of his firstborn. He worked long hours, traveled a lot on business, and drank too much scotch when he was home.

There was never any laughter in the house.

Eventually his mother got a job working as an aide at a private elementary school. He supposed she was looking for minds to nourish, minds that wouldn't disappoint her like his had.

She never seemed to find anyone who measured up to her memories of Justin.

Probably even Justin himself couldn't measure up to those memories, I thought.

As he talked, he was very far away, buried in a childhood that he had tried to outrun on the cross-country trails, or conquer in the classroom.

Finally, he was quiet.

And my heart ached for the boy who could never win.

Chapter 26

I finally broke the silence. "It's not your fault."

"Of course it's my fault," he said miserably.

"You are not responsible for the fact that your mother used you as a replacement for the child she lost rather than loving you in your own right."

"How could she love a failure?" he asked.

I wanted to argue with him, try to make him see the truth, but I realized that he had a whole lifetime of pain behind that statement, and he couldn't just suddenly throw all of that away and get on with his life.

"Most parents would be thrilled to have a son like you," I said.

He didn't believe me. "We'd better get started. It's getting late."

I don't know how long we talked, but the light that filtered through the curtain was softer now, more slanted.

And I knew that I couldn't leave with him. Somehow I think he knew that, too.

"I have to go," I said.

"No," he demanded, but there was more sadness than determination in his voice.

"I have to go," I repeated, getting up from the chair, feeling the stiff pain in my ankles. I must have been sitting motionless for hours, listening to him.

"Don't leave," he said.

"I have to," I said. "I have to go before they start looking for me. That way I can come back."

I think I meant it.

I headed for the door, not wanting to look back at him. If I just kept walking, calmly and normally, maybe he'd just let me go.

"Bethany."

I told myself not to look back, but I did. His hand was coming out of the deep bottom drawer of the desk, and in his hand was a gun. It was small and black, but I was not deceived by its size.

My eyes locked on his. "No," I said softly. "No."

Then I turned my back and began walking. Somewhere deep inside of me I believed that he wouldn't shoot me. That thought kept me walking down the stairs, through the living room and dining room, and back through the kitchen and out the door through which I'd entered this house hours and hours ago. I didn't run; I didn't listen for footsteps behind me. I simply walked out of there.

Once I felt the fresh air on my face, once I felt the crispness of the grass under my bare feet, that's when I started shaking.

I had to get away. I wasn't sure what I had to get away from the most.

It was either the possibility of being held against my will, or the possibility of hearing a sound that I did not want to hear.

Then I ran.

I ran through that backyard, and through the backyard that adjoined it, until I was on the street one block over from mine, and then I started down that block, knowing that my house was only a few blocks farther down.

As I neared the first corner, panting for breath, my ankles throbbing with pain that I barely acknowledged, I heard someone yell.

"Wolfgang, find Bethany. Find her, Wolfgang."

That's when I started to cry. Sure enough, Wolfgang came tearing around the corner. I don't know whether it was luck or tracking, but there he was. I knelt down on the sidewalk, and he ran to me, yipping joyously.

Then, around the corner ran Starling. His hair was all rumpled, and his glasses were slightly askew. He'd never looked better to me in his entire life.

"Good dog, Wolfgang," he said, racing down the sidewalk to join us. "You found Bethany."

Right. Just like Starling to give the dog all the credit. I'd have to straighten him out on that one.

Starling knelt down in front of me where Wolfgang was licking the tears that were falling down my face.

"Was it him?" he asked.

I nodded.

"Are you okay? Did he hurt you?"

Wordlessly I held out my wrists, which were caked with dried blood.

"Is he still around? We have to get you out of here," Starling said, pulling me gently to my feet.

That sounded good. We started down the street, Wolfgang leaping up at us and barking.

"When you weren't at graduation practice, I got worried," Starling said. "I went to your house and your car was there, but you weren't. Then I noticed that the front door wasn't closed tight, and when I found that it wasn't locked, I really got worried. I didn't figure you'd go out and leave it open. So I looked around the house but I didn't see anything, so I started searching around for you."

"You didn't see the heart?" I asked.

"What's wrong with your voice?" Starling asked. I just shook my head. "There was another heart? Where?"

"On the bathroom mirror," I said.

"He broke into your house?" Starling asked. I nodded.

"My car's a few blocks from your house," Starling said, his words running together. "We're going straight to the police. I talked to them once today but they said you didn't qualify as a missing person but now it's different and I called your father's company and got his number in California, but he'd already left for the airport in California but I know he'd want you to go straight to the police."

I stopped walking so abruptly that Wolfgang ran into me. This wasn't going to work. Everything in my brain told me that Starling was right. Get out of here. Go to the police. Finish this once and for all.

But another part of me said no. That part of me said that I'd never be able to live with what was going to happen.

And I knew that it was going to happen. Suddenly I knew as surely as I knew my own name.

"I'm sorry, Starling. I have to go back," I said, reversing direction and picking up the pace.

"What?" Starling bellowed. "You're going back to somebody who broke into your house and tied you up? You can't. I won't let you. This is ridiculous. Let the police deal with him."

"He has a gun," I said by way of explanation.

"Great. He has a gun. You're going back to some lunatic with a gun who will probably kill you. Bethany, you can't do this."

Starling grabbed my arm, and I threw him off.

"Bethany, has he brainwashed you? What is this?"

I didn't blame Starling for being confused, but I didn't know how to explain it. Instead, I took off at a run, back through the yards again, yards I'd never planned to cross again as long as I lived.

Wolfgang and Starling followed. Only Wolfgang was having a good time.

"Bethany, I won't let you do this. Your father would kill me if I let you do this."

"You can't stop me," I yelled over my shoulder. I started slowing down to a fast walk. I wasn't in very good shape for this much exercise, and my mind was racing. I didn't have much time.

I looked at Starling, and I could see that desperation had set in. He was probably about ready to tackle me, and if I ended up restrained one more time, I'd lose my sanity.

"He has a gun?" Starling screeched. "He has a gun, and you're going back in there?"

"He won't use it on me," I said, trying to reassure him, trying to reassure myself.

"Then why does he have it?" Starling panted.

"For himself," I answered, knowing I was right.

"Bethany, we'll call the police. They have people trained for this. SWAT teams. Psychiatrists. Let them handle it."

"There's not enough time," I yelled. In fact, it might already be too late.

"So what am I supposed to do?" Starling asked. "Stand around and listen for shots? Bethany, this isn't a good plan. Not good at all."

"I know," I admitted. Still, it was the only one I had. I explained it to Starling.

I rushed back into the house through the kitchen door, Starling behind me. I went up the steps, trying to mask the footsteps of Starling as he lagged behind me.

I went to the bedroom doorway. He was on the bed, the gun in his hand.

He sat up, startled, the gun waving.

"Bethany."

I walked toward him, suddenly losing confidence that my instincts were right. Maybe he would shoot me. Still, I had to get closer.

He pointed the gun in my direction, but he didn't say anything.

"You won't harm me," I said, and I don't know which of us I was trying to convince of that. I took another step toward him. Now I was only about three steps from the side of the bed.

"Go," he said. "Just go. That's what you wanted to do all along."

"Not without that."

"No," he said, but then his eyes swung to the doorway. In bounded Wolfgang. And in that instant, I lunged for the gun.

If he had really wanted to, he probably would have had time to shoot either me or himself, but he didn't. His eyes were glued to the bundle of fur that hurtled through the door and leaped against my legs.

By the time I looked up, Starling was in the doorway. I held out the gun to him, and he took it and left.

"It's over," I said.

He nodded.

"It will be okay," I repeated, over and over again. I sat on the edge of the bed because my legs wouldn't hold me up any longer. "It will be okay." We both started to cry as Wolfgang looked from one of us to the other in confusion.

Finally Wolfgang went to Brent and put his front feet on his chest and stared at him quizzically. Then he licked away the tears.

We were frozen in time, it seemed, until the sounds downstairs brought us back to reality. Two policemen soon filled the doorway, with Starling right behind them. I guess Starling had told them as much as he knew, because they seemed to know what to do.

"We'll need a statement from you," the first cop said.

I nodded, tears still streaming down my face.

"But your friend says that you have a prior engagement," the second cop added.

I looked at him, not understanding.

"Graduation?"

I had completely forgotten.

"We'll see you after the ceremony," he said, and they turned their attention to the young man on the bed.

I gathered up Wolfgang and headed for the door.

Starling and I walked down the steps and, once again, I left that house.

This time I knew I'd never be back.

"That was fast." I needed to break the silence.

"They were giving somebody a speeding ticket two blocks over while I was looking for somebody to let me use their phone," Starling explained. "I told them everything I knew."

"I really don't think he ever meant to hurt me," I reasoned.

"I'm just glad he didn't." Starling smiled a little and put his arm around me as we walked back to my house. Wolfgang lagged behind, his tongue hanging out, so I stopped to pick him up.

"I was just ready to create a diversion when Wolfgang got past me," Starling said.

"I'm sure you were." I smiled. "I knew you'd help."

"I just didn't want you to think that Wolfgang did it all on his own." Starling the hero.

"How did you end up with him, anyway?" I asked.

"When I was searching for you, I couldn't find anything to tell me where you were, what direction to go, anything. I was going crazy.

So I drove over to Mr. Baldwin's and grabbed Wolfgang, figuring maybe he could at least head me in the right direction."

"Does Mr. Baldwin know what's been going on?" I asked, suddenly concerned. He shouldn't be worrying.

"No," Starling answered. "All he knows is that I borrowed his dog rather abruptly."

Two blocks from my house was Starling's car. I had never been so glad in my life to see Dinosaur, huge body and all. Good old Starling. He still must have been trying to keep his distance and play spy.

"What time is it?" I suddenly asked.

Starling looked down at his watch. "Seven twenty-six."

"You have to hurry!" I said, shoving him toward the car.

"What do you mean, I have to hurry?"

"You have to get to graduation. You have to give the valedictory speech."

"You have to graduate, too."

"Starling, look at me. I'm not exactly dressed for a formal ceremony. Go. Hurry."

"Not without you."

"Fine. I'll ride over with you," I said, more to get him moving than anything else. I was relieved to see his cap and gown on the backseat. "Hurry up."

It was a good thing there weren't any more cops in the vicinity giving speeding tickets, because Starling broke a few laws on the way to school.

By the time we pulled into the parking lot, it was filled with cars but empty of people. All I cared about was that Starling give his speech. He didn't deserve to miss that because of me.

"Pull up there." I pointed to the sidewalk at the front door. There was a low grade in the curb where the handicapped access was. Starling pulled right up to the front steps. "Run," I said, seeing a very startled-looking policeman on traffic duty heading for us at a slow trot. "I'll explain."

"Come with me," Starling pleaded.

"No. I'm not going in like this." White boxers, a T-shirt that was covered with dirt and grass stains, bare feet, and blood didn't strike me as appropriate graduation apparel.

"At least listen from the back."

I didn't have time to argue with him. Besides, I didn't feel like dealing with the cop. Maybe I could find my father and sit with him.

I couldn't leave Wolfgang in the car, so I gathered him up along with Starling's cap and gown, and Starling and I took off again, up the front steps and into the school. We raced down the front hallway to the auditorium, and panted to a stop at the open doorway. A startled usher handing out programs gaped at us in amazement.

"You wear my gown," Starling said, trying to regain his breath.

"No," I said, throwing it over his head and perching the hat on top. I didn't know which way it was supposed to go.

Sitting on stage were the administrators, school board members, and a few other dignitaries I couldn't identify. The graduates were a sea of red gowns and caps in the front twenty or so rows, and the rest of the auditorium was filled to overflowing with families and friends.

The principal was at the podium, looking more grim than usual. "It is with great pride and satisfaction that I present to you this class, certifying that all of its members have met the requirements for graduation," he began. There were a few cheers from the front twenty rows.

"Tonight, the valedictory speech was scheduled to be given by Mr. Starling Horace Whitman the Fifth, the only member of the graduating class to have maintained a perfect 4.0 average. However . . ."

"Go," I said to Starling, giving him a push. He had to get started down the aisle before the principal cancelled him.

He went. There was only one problem.

He had me firmly by the hand, and he wouldn't let go.

SHE SAVED ME.
I KNEW SHE WAS PERFECT.
SOMEDAY I'LL BE OUT OF HERE.
SOMEDAY I'LL FIND HER AGAIN.
THE NEXT TIME . . .

About the Author

Jane McFann has written several books for young people, including *Maybe by Then I'll Understand, One More Chance,* and *One Step Short.* She lives and works in Delaware where she teaches English at Glasgow High School.

Ms. McFann enjoys teaching, writing, family, friends, rabbits, strawberries with whipped cream, tennis, flowers, and laughter.

THRILLERS

R.L. Stine

☐ MC44236-8 The Baby-sitter $3.50
☐ MC44332-1 The Baby-sitter II $3.50
☐ MC46099-4 The Baby-sitter III $3.50
☐ MC45386-6 Beach House $3.25
☐ MC43278-8 Beach Party $3.50
☐ MC43125-0 Blind Date $3.50
☐ MC43279-6 The Boyfriend $3.50
☐ MC44333-X The Girlfriend $3.50
☐ MC45385-8 Hit and Run $3.25
☐ MC46100-1 The Hitchhiker $3.50
☐ MC43280-X The Snowman $3.50
☐ MC43139-0 Twisted $3.50

Caroline B. Cooney

☐ MC44316-X The Cheerleader $3.25
☐ MC41641-3 The Fire $3.25
☐ MC43806-9 The Fog $3.25
☐ MC45681-4 Freeze Tag $3.25
☐ MC45402-1 The Perfume $3.25
☐ MC44884-6 The Return of the
Vampire $2.95
☐ MC41640-5 The Snow $3.25
☐ MC45682-2 The Vampire's
Promise $3.50

Diane Hoh

☐ MC44330-5 The Accident $3.25
☐ MC45401-3 The Fever $3.25
☐ MC43050-5 Funhouse $3.25
☐ MC44904-4 The Invitation $3.50
☐ MC45640-7 The Train $3.25

Sinclair Smith

☐ MC45063-8 The Waitress $2.95

Christopher Pike

☐ MC43014-9 Slumber Party $3.50
☐ MC44256-2 Weekend $3.50

A. Bates

☐ MC45829-9 The Dead
Game $3.25
☐ MC43291-5 Final Exam $3.25
☐ MC44582-0 Mother's Helper $3.50
☐ MC44238-4 Party Line $3.25

D.E. Athkins

☐ MC45246-0 Mirror, Mirror $3.25
☐ MC45349-1 The Ripper $3.25
☐ MC44941-9 Sister Dearest $2.95

Carol Ellis

☐ MC46411-6 Camp Fear $3.25
☐ MC44768-8 My Secret
Admirer $3.25
☐ MC46044-7 The Stepdaughter $3.25
☐ MC44916-8 The Window $2.95

Richie Tankersley Cusick

☐ MC43115-3 April Fools $3.25
☐ MC43203-6 The Lifeguard $3.25
☐ MC43114-5 Teacher's Pet $3.25
☐ MC44235-X Trick or Treat $3.25

Lael Littke

☐ MC44237-6 Prom Dress $3.25

Edited by T. Pines

☐ MC45256-8 Thirteen $3.50

Available wherever you buy books, or use this order form.